The Secret Twin

THE FOOL

The fool wavers on the precipice, frightened of stepping off or moving backward. The vista in front of him may be beautiful, but he cannot let go of the landscape behind him.

The Secret Twin

Denise Gosliner Orenstein

Katherine Tegen Books
An Imprint of HarperCollins*Publishers*

Also by
Denise Gosliner Orenstein

When the Wind Blows Hard
Unseen Companion

Excerpt on page 387 from "An Old Cracked Tune," from *The Collected Poems* by
Stanley Kunitz. Copyright © 2000 by Stanley Kunitz. Used by permission of W.W.
Norton & Company, Inc.

HarperTempest is an imprint of
HarperCollins Publishers.

The Secret Twin
Copyright © 2007 by Denise Gosliner Orenstein
Art by Dan McCarthy

www.harperteen.com

Library of Congress Cataloging-in-Publication Data
Orenstein, Denise Gosliner.
   The secret twin / Denise Gosliner Orenstein. — 1st ed.
      p.   cm.
   Summary: Born a conjoined twin, thirteen-year-old Noah bears the secret guilt
of being the only survivor, and now finds himself in the care of a stranger with a
secret of her own.
   ISBN-10: 0-06-078564-0 (trade bdg.) — ISBN-13: 978-0-06-078564-2 (trade bdg.)
   ISBN-10: 0-06-078565-9 (lib. bdg.) — ISBN-13: 978-0-06-078565-9 (lib. bdg.)
   [1. Emotional problems—Fiction. 2. Conjoined twins—Fiction. 3. Twins—
Fiction. 4. Secrets—Fiction.] I. Title.

PZ7.O6314Se 2007   2006003876
[Fic]—dc22   CIP
                                                                        AC

Typography by Christopher Stengel
1 2 3 4 5 6 7 8 9 10
❖
First Edition

For Kathy Jane Gosliner:
sister, comforter, whisperer, listener, secret sharer . . .

"Closer to me than my bones"
—Franz Wright, *Flight*

·CONTENTS·

I will pioneer a new way, explore unknown powers, and unfold to the world the deepest mysteries of creation.

—*Frankenstein*, Mary Shelley

The Tarot is an excellent method for turning human experience into wisdom. At its essence, the Tarot deals with archetypal symbols of the human situation, symbols one can relate to our own lives and that help us better understand ourselves.

—*Tarot Plain and Simple*, Anthony Louis

The Death Card represents new beginnings as
well as letting go of the past.

NOAH

They say the newborn don't see, but I remember this:

Your eyelids were ruffled.
I think you whimpered once, a crumpled cough,
then opened your tiny mouth again
dribbling pretty foam.
Your breath was embalmed with milk:
    sticky sweet.

You saw me too.

WEEK ONE

THE DEVIL

This image represents our tendency to remain chained
to personal history and our inabilities to move forward in
our lives. The devil keeps us imprisoned in the dark,
bolting every door and locking every window.

Surgery makes me nervous.

Thank goodness, Mademoiselle's face-lift is complete.

Both the doctor and Nurse Grace finally call at 6:00 p.m. and 6:10 p.m., then again later, which gives me enough time to prepare the bedroom for her return.

I stretch the ivory sheets across the queen-size bed and smooth her cream velveteen comforter until every wrinkle disappears. Mademoiselle and I like the palest of palettes throughout.

Everything will have to be just so, as if she had never been away at all, and as she requested before leaving for the hospital in the morning.

Mademoiselle's black silk mules are right by

the chaise, just where she likes them, along with a stack of her favorite newspapers and magazines. My grandmother was a showgirl in her younger days, and still likes to keep abreast of all the fashions and styles. Sometimes she asks me to sit by her when looking at the magazine photographs and help pick out hairstyles that might suit her face and outfits that would be most flattering on her small frame.

I even remember to insert the tape of *What Ever Happened to Baby Jane?* in the VCR, Mademoiselle's favorite black-and-white film. We think she favors Joan Crawford when the actress was still very slim.

Everyone is surprised that I am Mademoiselle's thirteen-year-old grandson, and that she is almost eighty years old. It is generally thought that both of us are younger than our actual ages, since I am fairly short and extremely thin and Mademoiselle keeps herself in the best possible condition, drinking eight glasses of water and ingesting a maximum of 1,000 calories per day.

Although I would never dare tell her so, I think my grandmother's hair gives her age away, since it is thinning and splitting at the ends from years and years of being dyed deep black. She used to keep her hair in a permanent "up" do, teased and plastered and at least six inches high, but she has recently adopted a more youthful style, wearing it down all the time at my suggestion. It is true that the ends frizz in humidity, but my grandmother stays inside most of the time anyway, and the shorter cut gives her a more contemporary look.

Mademoiselle is my only grandmother and I have lived with her ever since my parents were killed in a car crash when I was four years old. They say you can't remember much of anything that far back, but I still can feel the dizziness of being held in some stranger's arms, and how different it felt once I began living with Mademoiselle.

After all, a child should by raised by his own flesh and blood.

I am also different from children my age in many other ways, disliked and avoided at school. This is a fact I accept, that no longer bothers me; it is sometimes even a comfort, since I am usually left alone. I know that I am thought to be strange, called names, and often even pushed around. But when I see them coming, when I see that look in their eyes or hear those ugly, distorted words, I know to disappear.

I know just how to vanish within.

I am aware that I am unusual and not like anyone else. I am really only half a boy, although no one knows anything about that.

Sometimes I imagine how my classmates would react if they knew the real, whole story of my life, particularly the circumstances surrounding my birth.

The surprising thing to most is that I like girls quite a significant amount; at least I am sure about this one particular fact. Perhaps, because of my formal bearing and commitment to an impeccable appearance, an assumption of something else is often made. Even Mademoiselle asked me outright one evening while we were watching an old movie on TV starring Cary Grant.

"You know, my darling," she said softly, fingering her satin bed jacket with a white-gloved hand, "I would not actually mind having a fancy boy as a grandson. In fact, it might prove to be quite interesting and would not bother me in the very least." She dabbed at her lips with an embroidered lace handkerchief and smiled at me again. "I always thought your great-uncle Sebie was one of them, but unfortunately he died before I ever got to the bottom of that." Mademoiselle always slathers her elbows with moisturizer at night and wears perfectly fresh white cotton gloves. I have always admired her attention to grooming and her meticulous nature, as these are qualities that we both share.

"I am certain that I am not a fancy boy," I told Mademoiselle in the calmest of tones. It didn't bother me one bit that she thought so; I already knew she had suspicions by certain references she made and by the way she looked at me when I admired the slight sequined gowns hanging in her closet. "From what I understand," I continued, fluffing up her pillow just the way she liked, "I would know it if that was my preference—a leaning clearly evident from the start."

"Hmm," she murmured, shifting under her

covers. Mademoiselle is a tiny slip of a woman, and she sometimes looks like a child under the mound of blankets and comforters on her large four-poster bed. "I suppose that is so."

And the subject never came up between us again. I do think I would know if I liked boys, but to tell the truth, girls interest me a bit more. I like the scent of them when they whiz past me in the hall, how their skin shimmers; and I am apt to look all over them, from their very toes all the way up to you-know-what. I am not obsessed, however, not like the rest of the boys. Actually, at this point in my life, other things are more of a concern to me, more of a priority right now.

But secretly, sometimes I wish I had been born different in that one particular way.

At least there is a community for that.

"We must keep Mademoiselle's door shut at all times and both her room and the rest of the house perfectly quiet," I whisper to Nurse Grace after she arrives, keeping my eyes lowered so that all I see is the tangle of soiled laces on her wide white sneakers. Imitation leather, I can tell that right off. Both heels are worn down at the sides, and her feet seem huge, swollen and spilling out all over at the ankles.

I have never seen such a large woman in my whole life. Or should I refer to her as a girl? She is clearly quite young, maybe in her late twenties or early thirties, although it is difficult to tell because of her size, and I find myself staring at her freckled, rawboned hands and the way her flesh dimples at her wrists. I do not look up at her enormous face.

Her shadow takes up the entire floor.

She is at least three times the size of Mademoiselle—maybe Mademoiselle and I put together and then doubled twice over again.

She must weigh over two hundred pounds, I think, careful not to utter a word.

The double of a woman might just flatten half a boy.

Of course, my eyes are lowered. It's hard to tell a lot from a shoe.

Nurse Grace nods. "If you wish," she responds softly. "I'll try to take my cues from you since you'll know what will be best."

I am immediately grateful that she understands exactly who is in charge.

"Maybe you could show me my room,
Noah," I hear her voice drift toward me. "I've
been instructed where you and your grandmother sleep, but would you mind showing me
where I should put all of my stuff and where I'm
going to stay?"

I make sure to keep my head down as I lead
her up the soft stairway, worried that Nurse
Grace's enormous white shoes, padded with ridged
rubber soles, will leave footprints on the carpet.

Poor Mademoiselle would certainly have
none of that.

But for now, more important things are on
my mind. I am concentrating on getting this huge
girl out of my way. I have enough to deal with. I
am not interested in talking to her and becoming
friends of any kind. All I want is to avoid thinking about my grandmother's painful surgery and
to be left completely alone. I can even picture
Mademoiselle sleeping behind her bedroom door
and, for a moment, hear her gentle snoring. But

of course, that is impossible. Mademoiselle always reminded me that she has never been known to snore.

That first evening Nurse Grace arrives is peculiar at best. I sit on the bed in my darkened room, somehow overcome with an undefinable foreboding. The usual order of my own home is disrupted, and a complete stranger, someone whom I really know nothing about, is taking over the household, a job usually left entirely up to me. I listen to muffled sounds coming from the next room and imagine Nurse Grace sitting by Mademoiselle's side, watching for a rise in temperature or an infection.

How does one determine when infection sets in? I wonder, suddenly alarmed. What if everything in my carefully organized life is changed on the largest of possible scales? What if this household is never to be the same again? I hold my breath for a moment and listen to heavy footsteps at my door.

"Noah?" Nurse Grace's voice is childlike, almost musical, without any of the heft befitting her size. "Now that I've finished my chores, would you like some dinner? May I come in?"

"Yes, of course," I reply quietly, although this is the last thing in the world that I would like. "Come inside if you desire."

I have always been taught that rudeness is unnecessary. Mademoiselle would not approve of that.

I hear the door creak open, but I keep my head down, staring at the white plush carpet and then shifting my eyes over to Nurse Grace's colossal feet. She has taken off her sneakers and is wearing what are commonly known as Hush Puppies, faux suede oxfords that look as though they belong on a man. Two thick pink calves protrude like small shoulders of meat, wrapped in a kind of shiny, transparent material, something I recognize as support hose, an item of intimate apparel in which Mademoiselle would absolutely never be caught dead.

"How common, how ordinary," my grandmother would say as we watched commercials for women's hose on television. "Silk stockings are the only proper choice. One's attire should always be flawless, my darling—make sure that you never forget that. The end always justifies the means, dearest child, and no matter the discomfort, one's appearance must always come first."

How often had I heard my grandmother say this very same thing? That appearance must take precedence over comfort, guise over honesty and contentment?

It was only later in my life that I really understood what she meant.

"Was she in dreadful pain?" I finally hear myself ask Nurse Grace. "Was she conscious? Did she know what was happening the entire time?"

I hate to think of Mademoiselle all alone on that hospital gurney, probably ignored by doctors and nurses alike. A face-lift is considered a vanity surgery, and she probably did not get any sympathy from anyone.

It pains me to think of my grandmother suffering or frightened, even a little bit.

Nurse Grace sits down on the bed next to me; I hear the mattress squeak and I hold on tightly so that her weight will not pull me right over to her side. I see a hem ribbed with small bouquets of rosy flowers fluttering on her impossibly large lap. The smell of something aromatic is on her breath, as if she has been sucking on a hard candy, butterscotch, or some other flavor difficult to pinpoint, sweet coconut or vanilla.

"She didn't suffer, Noah. She wasn't awake at all. I know how much your grandmother means to you, and how very difficult this must be. I know that there aren't any relatives to help out and that you must deal with much of this all alone. Maybe my being here for a while will help make it easier. Just until things are back to normal. Anyway, it might be good for you to talk about it. When you're ready, that is."

"Does she have many scars? Does she look different or the same?"

Strangely enough, despite the situation, it is somehow important to me that Mademoiselle's scars are minimal, that she was not cut up too badly or disfigured. I simply cannot bear to think of her like that.

My grandmother was always made up so

perfectly, particularly in her younger years, her eyebrows drawn in a careful arch, thick foundation applied from forehead to chin, and rouge dotting her checks, just as if she had been thoroughly kissed. Only her bright lipstick was slightly off the mark, often sticking to her teeth like tiny bits of red confetti. And then, of course, as she aged, the precision of application, her attention to detail, was sometimes overlooked.

Still, I find that the idea of her face marred in any way disturbs me a great deal.

"I haven't seen her myself, but I'm sure there are hardly any marks. Don't worry, I'm certain your grandmother will look as you remember her." Nurse Grace's voice is annoyingly gentle, almost cloying.

I shrug.

I wish she would leave me alone again in my very own room.

"You must be hungry," I hear her say as she suddenly stands up, so that I topple over onto my left side. "Come on downstairs and let's see what we can find for me to make for dinner."

"No, thank you."

I study my hands. Mademoiselle had just buffed my nails the week before and they shine like tiny slivers of light. "We usually do not eat much of an evening supper, Mademoiselle and myself. We believe that it is best to have the heartier meal at lunchtime so as to properly digest. It is not that beneficial to eat so close to bedtime."

"But you're a growing boy." Her voice is stronger now and I see her feet shift position. "You need fuel to keep your body healthy and strong."

What Nurse Grace does not know is this: Half a boy needs little nourishment in order to survive.

· DAY TWO ·

NOAH

The odor of eggs and bacon wakes me the next morning and I am alarmed.

For a moment, I forget that Nurse Grace has moved in and wonder who in the world is making such a commotion downstairs. I sit up in bed, holding on to the pile of books at my side so that they do not slide onto the floor.

Then I remember. All about Mademoiselle's surgery and about the monstrous stranger who has moved into our small house.

The sun streaks through the narrow window opposite me, warming my books and making the top volume almost too hot to touch. Despite the heat, I shiver, feeling goose bumps rise on my arms and chest.

My tan terry cloth slippers are at the foot of

the bed and I slip them on carefully, then swing my legs together to the floor as if they are one. Often I test my own agility by trying to see if I can move my limbs in unison, pretending them to be attached by an invisible cord. Sometimes I will hop across the room like this, in a kind of one-legged limp, attempting to determine how long I might survive with such a handicap, as if I had been disfigured in this manner from birth.

Something not so far from the truth.

Just a silly test of some sort, my clumsy lunging across the floor, a game I play when alone in the privacy of my own room.

Nothing I ever let anyone else know about or see.

That is certain. That is for sure.

There is a rustling in the kitchen downstairs and then a loud bang, the sound of a pan or plate falling to the floor. I sigh, anxious that the house remain quiet.

Nurse Grace must be preparing breakfast, taking over my very own job, and I shudder, the scent of food making me nauseous.

Of course, the stranger downstairs in my

small kitchen has no way of knowing, but Mademoiselle and I like our breakfast just so, and I usually bring it upstairs on a white ceramic tray, the one with little legs, so that my grandmother can eat and still watch TV. She does not drink coffee nor will she eat white sugar or anything made with processed flour. Twice a week, a small cube of butter is allowed on her oatmeal, and egg yolks are altogether banned. Once, long ago, I made Mademoiselle cinnamon toast, just for something different, but I certainly got an earful about that.

"You know, my darling," she said, pushing the tray away, "refined sugar and refined flour are a lethal combination. What on earth gave you an idea to make something this toxic?"

I felt absolutely mortified at the time, and whisked Mademoiselle's breakfast tray right off the bed. I returned promptly with a bowl of frozen strawberries marinated in red wine and made a mental note to dispose of any white food that might still be in the house.

Mademoiselle rarely had very harsh words for me. She managed to let me know her likes and dislikes with a look, a disdainful glance, or even a delicate sniffle as she looked away. My grandmother had the most marvelous of manners and I intend to learn as much from her as I am humanly able.

But now, an enormous Nurse Grace is bumbling her way around our immaculate kitchen, dropping pans and probably stirring up all kinds of ingredients brimming with cholesterol and saturated fats. Of course there is nothing to be done about it, but I yearn to give her a piece of my mind and take over my usual responsibilities.

Mornings, on summer days such as this, at about 10:00 A.M., I would usually rouse slowly and then head downstairs to the kitchen in my freshly pressed robe. I would make Mademoiselle her favorite breakfast of egg white omelet with just a touch of cheddar cheese and pink grapefruit cut into exact quarters.

All would seem perfectly normal then.

Sometimes I would pick some artificial baby's breath from the silk bouquet by the sink, and fold my grandmother's embossed paper napkin three ways to make a perfectly simulated tulip.

Each morning I marched up the white carpeted stairs, careful not to wake her until I opened the door, then I would flip the switch connected to the light and her radio, and wait for the blare of music to begin. Always the same song, her preference, "Learn to Be Lonely," from the *Phantom of the Opera* soundtrack. And Mademoiselle would stretch her slim arms as far as they could go and whip off her satin eye mask in a motion just like the dancer she once was. Then she would sit up and say in her high-pitched voice, "Good morning, my dear. I hope that you had a pleasant rest."

Mademoiselle almost never woke up grumpy. She was mostly content, unless her slumber had been disturbed during the night, and she was usually satisfied with the breakfast I had prepared.

Of course, there were exceptions. No one is perfect, after all.

Mornings, I would forget about the noises and the ghosts that had followed me in my own sleep. I would forget about the nightmares, the sounds at the windows, the clawing at my door.

At daylight, when I would bring Mademoiselle her breakfast tray and watch as she sat up in bed, the shadows would begin to disappear, and I would feel almost like a whole boy.

I would know what each day would bring and exactly what to expect.

All that is changed now. Poor Mademoiselle is overcome with a deep sleep, and a complete stranger is touching each and every one of our personal belongings, all of our most private, hidden things.

The unexpected now licks its greedy lips and extends its hands, twisting what I have always known completely upside down.

After breakfast, I feel sick.

I sit at the kitchen table, staring at my cereal bowl and wishing it to disappear. Nurse Grace has insisted that I finish my gray glob of oatmeal, and I feel the sticky stuff roll inside my stomach in a solid lump. She looks up at me and smiles brilliantly, clearly pleased with herself, then turns back to the gargantuan meal spread all over her plate.

I find it impossible to tear my eyes away, as if eyewitness to a lurid crime, somehow compelled to watch her relentlessly gobble up a greasy plate of fried bacon and eggs. Somehow I am fascinated as the woman's broad, speckled hand shovels forkfuls from the plate to her mouth again and again. She has buttered some toast and the oil dribbles into the crevices between her fingers. Does this stop her relentless rampage? No. Determined, she finishes every single morsel and then has the audacity to clean her plate with a soggy corner of bread.

I pray she washes her hands before touching anything else in the house that Mademoiselle has been so careful to keep immaculate.

Luckily, Nurse Grace soaps up the dishes by hand, swaying over a sinkful of hot bubbles and wiping her face with a handkerchief. I do not care to think about where that handkerchief has been before or where it might end up.

"Hand me a towel, will you, Noah?" she asks, as if I have any choice.

Oddly enough, to tell the truth, Mademoiselle and I rarely use the real china, but content ourselves with paper plates. This may seem strange for a woman of such high standards, but my grandmother often insisted that it made no sense to be puckering up our hands in common dishwater. Skin ages quickly.

"Let's just use the disposable ones, my darling," she would say with a smile, waving a slender hand in the air. "It is really more sanitary, anyway."

I definitely had no problem with that.

Clearly this will not do for Nurse Grace, and to make matters even worse, just as I am preparing an escape upstairs, to lie down in my own room until the nervous stomach passes, she takes me by the elbow without any warning.

I flinch.

I am not used to being touched by anyone at all.

"Come sit with me for a moment," she says, blocking the stairway with her incredible bulk. "I picked up the newspaper from the stoop outside. We can read it together on the couch if you like. I think I saw a section of comics—the colored ones, in fact."

"I prefer not to chat while reading," I reply, insulted about the allusion to comics, while assessing a means to make my getaway. But she just laughs, pointing to the living room and giving me practically no choice at all.

But when she refuses to keep quiet and has the audacity to keep reading the news out loud, when she begins to discuss a neighborhood shooting reported in the paper today, then neglects to respond to my inquiries at all, when she continues to ask me personal questions, none of which are any of her business in the first place, it is not long before I start desperately plotting my exit.

"Excuse me," I finally interrupt, "but I have reading of my own that must be completed upstairs. I am afraid that I must spend the rest of the day in my room."

"The rest of the day?" I can hear the disappointment in her voice. "What's so important that you have to spend all day upstairs? Stay here with me for a while, Noah. Let's take the time to get to know one another."

I lose my patience then. Is it my job to keep

this woman occupied at the expense of my own, carefully established routines? No. I have no interest in getting to know Nurse Grace or forming a relationship of any kind. Each and every summer day, once Mademoiselle has finished her breakfast and I have washed the dishes downstairs, I am allowed the afternoon to myself, something I cherish fervently. And the last thing I wish to endure is a thorough questioning of my life. There is nothing that Nurse Grace needs to know about me, nothing I ever intend to share.

In any case, shouldn't Nurse Grace be tending to things in Mademoiselle's room?

I stand up, but then do not know exactly what to say. So, although I am aware of acting uncharacteristically rude, I simply turn around without another word and quickly head toward the stairs.

Before I know it, before she has a chance to object, I am safely ensconced in my own little bedroom.

This is the worst example of bad manners. Believe me, I am perfectly aware of that. I have been brought up to be polite, considerate, but there is only so much that a boy can take.

I don't know exactly what comes over me, but I simply cannot bear Nurse Grace's intrusive company one minute more.

I sit on my bed upstairs, feeling a bit ashamed about my recent behavior and overcome by a familiar dread.

Sometimes I feel such a strong compulsion to be alone, to escape scrutiny, to avoid any questioning or opportunity for others to discover the truth, that I think I will never again leave this small room. But the consequences of this would be disastrous in more ways than one, and I recognize the danger of my always being left alone with my distressing thoughts.

It is during those times of isolation, the moments when I am entirely by myself, that the old fears return, leaving narrow footprints on my back.

A familiar dread squeezes me again and again, making it difficult to breathe.

When alone, I cannot always keep dark

thoughts at bay, and begin to wonder, all over again, about my own birth and my twin, and about my brother's recorded death.

You see, I have a secret that involves my double and our infancy.

A half a boy can be born only in the most extraordinary of circumstances.

Such a birthright is mine.

My brother and I were delivered on April 1, 1989, and the date's irony is not lost on either Mademoiselle or myself.

We were born conjoined, face-to-face, sharing one heart, nourished by the same bloodstream, but both having two legs, two arms, and two pelvises.

He was the weaker twin.

He had difficulty sucking and in opening his little eyes.

His life depended on my heart pumping for us both; he had no strength of his own, and his mind was curdled, undeveloped, so I'm told.

His lungs were weak.

He faltered while I did not.

We were thoracopagus twins, from the Greek word *pagos*: "that which is fixed."

Fixed to one another, we were meant to remain conjoined forever.

Thoracopagus twins are always involved in the sharing of the heart.

We are the rarest of human beings.

But not long after our birth, I'm told, they let him die: my brother, my twin. They called it "sacrifice surgery," they called him a "parasite aggressor," sapping my lifeblood until there would be nothing more.

They said we could not both survive.

They said a choice would have to be made.

Soon it would be all over for one of us, him or me.

They detached us at the heart, and at the bone, severing the bridge of human tissue that connected us both, pioneering new surgery, creating a new being and discarding another one.

So I'm told.

I am really just half a boy who wonders where his other half has disappeared. If you don't believe in heaven or hell, you will wonder exactly where your brother has gone.

Neither Mademoiselle nor I are religious, although we don't criticize those who are. We both believe in the here and now, and that there probably is not anything else. Still, once you are part of one whole, it is hard to imagine that your other half has simply vanished into thin air.

I wonder what they did with his body. Did they wrap him in a tiny blanket and build a coffin no bigger than my hand? Did they scrape him off the table with a giant scalpel, like a chef with so many pieces of gristle and bone? Did they x-ray his little body for science, examine each cell? Did he fight to breathe or did he simply give in?

These are questions that keep me up at night and seep into my dreams but I have never asked anyone for answers. Even Mademoiselle. It is clear that she does not care to talk about it, and I am not sure that I really want to know.

But sometimes, I secretly wonder: could it be that my twin brother somehow survived without my knowing? Could he be living somewhere else without a real family of his own? Is it possible that one day we might be reunited, two halves forming a whole? Does he know that he has another and does he yearn for me? Is he sad or content?

I just don't know.

And is it unnatural for a boy to ask such questions and not accept what he has always been told?

But these are simply private thoughts, hidden completely from view.

During one of her first telephone calls from her office on the evening of my grandmother's operation, Nurse Grace had told me she would stay at the house for a while to help with the aftermath of the surgery. Long before the actual event, Mademoiselle convinced me that she would need some professional assistance at home afterward and that someone would move in to help until she was healed. I did not like the sound of this at first, uncomfortable with the idea of a stranger in our midst. But since I do get queasy at the thought of blood or incisions, and of course have no experience with taking care of the infirm, we agreed it might be necessary for a short while. A professional nurse seemed the perfect solution, but Mademoiselle was quick to understand my apprehensions.

"Not to worry, my dear," my grandmother consoled me when she saw that I was anxious, "I'll make sure her references are impeccable, and I'll be certain to tell her to leave you absolutely all alone."

Mademoiselle may not be the most demonstrative grandmother in the world—she is not one to kiss or hug at all—but she understands my complex nature and is as considerate as she knows how to be. She is aware that I have a secret, one that we are both compelled to hide.

It is hard work staying silent, keeping certain words at bay. Sometimes the unspoken is insolent, crowding my mouth with words and stinging my tongue until I have to look the other way. But Mademoiselle is clearly uncomfortable with tears and I have learned how to swallow hard at any necessary moment of the day.

It is not easy being half a boy.

It is not easy to keep a secret, to keep your

real life hidden, underground.

No one knows that I am one of two brothers, and that there is a scar all the way down my chest, shaped like a rectangular box and protruding slightly where the surgeons stretched my skin to cover the gaping wound. I am told that a baby's flesh is flexible, easily molded into shape. It is not until later that the scars become permanent, a detailed map of what took place.

When I undress at night, I never look at my own flesh, at the large mound of elevated scars; I never look down.

My thoughts might seem very odd, even quite peculiar or insane. I am certain that I am not crazy, at least in the clinical sense, but I cannot help but wonder, and have, as long as I can remember: Could my twin's shadow be secretly at large?

I do not know of a witness to his murder; what I have heard has been passed down by those who were never even there.

This idea is not as far-fetched as it sounds. For a long time I have had the sense that my twin brother might still be skulking about. And although there is nothing specific, nothing particular at all—more of a feeling, an idea—for a long time I have had a premonition that everything might not be as it seems. Perhaps, after all, what I was told is not the truth.

One often hears of cases in which a newborn has vanished—been stolen, kidnapped, sold to another on the black market, even confused with another infant or switched soon after birth for personal gain. Unfortunately, they are more common than one might think. Could it not be possible that my double actually survived instead of perished, whisked off by some desperate nurse, or under another's starched white coat? It is clear that the surgery pushed the limits, created new boundaries, new laws for human life, so why not something else unexpected?

Two lives saved instead of one.

I have never even seen a death certificate, something Mademoiselle refuses to discuss. But in some ways my grandmother is quite innocent, unprepared to think the worst.

And perhaps, just perhaps, there is another somewhere with my face and my physique.

Could there still be two of me: one here in this little house, and the other wandering the earth, abandoned, bewildered, and alone?

For many years, lying in my bed at night and listening to Mademoiselle snoring in the next room, I would hear the floor creak below and the windows rattle. Nothing unusual, I suppose, but still, it was as if I heard his footsteps, saw his tiny hand at the window frame, sometimes his small shadow at the door. Silly things, ordinary things that worry all children in their dreams and in the dark.

Such as when a door blows shut for no apparent reason, when a cup of milk left on the counter suddenly disappears, when you cannot find the blue shirt you took pains to starch and hang in your closet the day before, when your heart pumps faster and faster, and when you are just plain scared.

But for me it was different. The wind had a face, the shadows a profile, each rattle a foot, each whisper a mouth. I told no one. No one would ever know. Insanity does not run in my family, and I had no interest in being considered a raving madman now or then. I knew I was not crazy. But I also had the distinct feeling that something else was wandering somewhere out there, maybe lost and alone. Perhaps he was angry, perhaps he was furious at being forgotten, all by himself with no one to care for him. I have had these thoughts for years and years and can tell no one.

I can never tell anyone. That is absolutely for sure.

And so the vaguest of ideas begin to hatch inside my head. At first these thoughts are completely obscure, without definition, just ideas without words, pictures without frames. At night, when I close my eyes, I hear voices calling, but I cannot understand what is being said; even during daylight, something pulls at me, but I have no idea of where to go. I am distracted, nervous, not myself at all.

It is the neighborhood shooting that provokes me, although I am not quite sure why. Somehow it instigates an internal chain of events, a reaction within. Why? I am not certain, but once hearing of the frightful crime, I find the need to learn more and more, almost obsessed with the thought of it, of someone being attacked nearby. What kind of person would do such a thing? What might be his motive, his state of mind? For some reason that I do not completely understand, I find that I am driven to learn more and more about the offense, the facts and details as they are uncovered, the mystery of the crime consuming my thoughts.

At the same time I am aware that a specter continues to haunt me, growing larger, always, always at my door.

I begin to wonder, could it possibly be my own twin who is hiding and acting out his terrible revenge?

· DAY ONE ·

GRACE

She's completely taken aback by the boy's fragility, his thin frame and pale skin. It's almost as if she can see right through the flesh to his veins, even to his very bones. As though he has never been fed properly, certainly not well cared for, a kid all on his own.

His eyes are sunken, his cheeks carved hollow, making his slightly hooked nose appear shockingly long against the angles of his face. The wide mouth is set in a permanent grimace, his lips are so tightly clamped together that they are practically invisible, creating the impression of toothlessness. Not exactly a handsome boy, in fact, pretty darn homely when you get down to it, and unfriendly to boot. Isn't it just her luck.

The pupils of the boy's eyes are the only

thing about him that looks really alive—two black specks darting nervously back and forth above his cheekbones, as if unsure what to finally focus on. Grace thinks of the Saturday morning cartoons that she watched with her little brother and the animated characters with invisible silhouettes whose movements across the screen could be tracked only by the progress of two restless, sooty eyes.

His head is shaven, which, combined with a bony frame, gives him the look of a victim. And his ears seem unusually large, out of proportion with the rest of his thin face. It's almost as though those ears are creatures of their own, enormous white butterflies, temporarily settling on the sides of his head but capable of surviving on their own.

Grace shivers.

Maybe the boy hasn't been sleeping; she's already noticed that he doesn't want to eat. Grace studies his stern expression and wonders if some extra pounds would transform him, make him look like a normal teenage boy instead of a ghost. Not some shadow of himself. But then who is she kidding, anyway. She's not exactly an expert in the matter. After all, she's not that far from being a teenager herself, only just turned twenty-one—this her very first position on location, her supervisor approving the assignment only because the office had been overcommitted and understaffed.

"Grace," Mrs. Saville had lectured her sternly, staring over the pair of bent eyeglass frames perched crookedly on her nose, a pile of papers scattered against the lopsided, dusty desk. "This is your chance to prove yourself, but I will be checking on the case's progress each and every day. You realize," her voice lowered suddenly and her glasses slipped so far down that Grace expected them to topple to the floor, "that this is a highly irregular placement. You are still certified only for day work, but this case doesn't appear to be particularly complicated or demand highly specialized skills. It's really just a matter of giving competent care, making sure the household runs well and that all needs are met thoroughly and efficiently. Of course, the situation is a somewhat sensitive matter, but it should be short-term. Since we have already gone over all of the details, I won't take up more of your time, but you realize, don't you, that there is a young boy involved, a thirteen-year-old, I believe."

Grace had known this. She had been given a three-page written report and spent the previous afternoon going over all the details of the case with Mrs. Saville, something that had annoyed Grace to no end. After all, it wasn't as if she was an idiot—she could read as well as anyone else. As if reading Grace's mind, the older woman had scowled. "Our agency has a reputation to pre-serve," she had said slowly, taking off her glasses and wiping her eyes as if suddenly tired, "and I expect the best from everyone in our employ."

Grace had tried to sit up straight and look confident, but she felt her hands shake and so she had looked down at her own feet.

Now that she is finally here, in this strange little white house, she must do as instructed, prove herself capable. This is her chance, and Grace is determined that no one question her experience or authority. She must stay in control of the household and of this odd boy.

Certainly, the situation is extremely touchy and she knows it's important not to overstep her bounds. He's a skittish boy, and hasn't even raised his head to look directly up at her; he tiptoes around the house, hunched over, long thin arms dangling at his sides, practically detached at the sockets. When she approaches, he backs himself up like a stray animal, as if he's never been exposed to human contact. Of course she knows this isn't the case, that the grandmother and the boy have been very close, at least according to the records. Even if his behavior is aggravating, she promises herself to keep a distance until he feels more comfortable, at least until he looks at her and asks directly for her help. She hopes that this won't take long.

But it will be only a week or so that she'll be here anyway. Grace sighs. Hardly enough time to really accomplish much of anything or establish much of a relationship at all. And there's nothing to rush back home for, nothing or no one waiting for her there. She thinks of her mother's small, cramped apartment across town and sighs again;

as usual, Grace had procrastinated, waiting until the last minute to pack her bag, barely having time to rush out the door, leaving clothes all over the bedroom floor, drawers half spilling over with assorted clothing, open boxes of doughnuts and crackers on the kitchen counter, dishes in the sink, newspapers and magazines scattered all over the floor. And, also as usual, her mother had been working late at the Cave, a small coffee shop where she waited on college kids who sat around all night in the booths, smoking and drinking herb tea but never leaving tips. Her mother rarely had time to clean the apartment, being too tired to care, coming home at 2:00 A.M. or later and collapsing into bed. Grace knows that she should do a better job helping her mother at home, but since neither of them really seemed to mind the mess, why bother?

Grace has resigned herself to the fact that she's become a full-fledged slob, forgetful about details and too lazy to help keep a well-ordered, proper home. Who would even know, who would even notice? They never have visitors stopping by and certainly don't have guests over for dinner anymore. It's even been a long time since any of Grace's friends have called.

So it's quite a shock to find herself in this new environment, this small brick house that's cleaner than immaculate, meticulous in ways she couldn't even imagine. Every single room's painted a different shade of white; the foyer in cream, the small dining room an eggshell, and the kitchen a darker ivory. Even the carpet's white, and extends all the way from the front door to the upstairs, then again from the triangular landing into each and every one of the three bedrooms. She wonders how it's kept perfectly clean. Not a smudge, not a footprint. As if no one really lives there at all, nobody ever underfoot. Only the hallway bathroom and the kitchen aren't carpeted, their floors covered in light linoleum, small haphazard white squares that don't seem to make any particular pattern at all. The three upstairs bedrooms are the same milky color, a cross between ivory and beige. All of the walls are blank, not a single shelf or picture hanging, just expanses of empty space. The entire house makes her head spin.

The grandmother's door remains tightly shut and Grace notices how the boy is careful to tiptoe each time he passes the room. She reminds herself to check all of the bedrooms later for laundry, linens and towels and the like. She sighs. Hauling around laundry baskets all day isn't exactly her idea of a good time.

And despite the fact that Grace's own apartment is much smaller, this house seems tiny, almost miniature, and she feels clumsy unpacking her old green suitcase on the twin bed. Her room here is little, there's no question about that, but something else about this house bugs her, makes her feel entirely out of place. It's too small, too bright, too confining, and her own bulk seems underscored: a large body stomping through a shrunken universe; an enormous, clumsy girl's hand trying to place the dainty furniture inside a child's dollhouse. There's an entirely different scale here and it's not one suited to her own size, that's for sure.

Grace pulls open the top bureau drawer. It's lined with tan shelf paper; there's a small crinoline sachet at the corner, lacking any fragrance at all. The other three drawers are exactly alike and she wonders how on earth she will fit all of her clothes into them: hooded sweatshirts, long T-shirts—even her underwear seems too large, too wide.

Her hand trembles as she looks down at the silver-framed photograph she's holding with both hands.

The glass is smudged and she wipes it with her shirt cuff, staring at the picture of a child. He's wearing a yellow rain slicker and carries a blue bucket in his arms. She swallows and looks back at the suitcase. It's half open, one sleeve from her favorite black sweatshirt, the one torn at the hem, flopped over the side as if part of a forgotten body. A corpse hidden from view.

Stop it.

She promised herself not to think this way anymore.

It's been a long time, just over two years, and look how far the grieving has gotten her.

Nowhere. Less than nowhere.

He was four, her only brother. His name was Liam.

Her mother had divorced her third husband by then. Liam's father. A burly, sullen man who disappeared after the accident. Nobody even tried contacting him. In reality, he'd been married to Grace's mother for a mere thirteen months. Who cared, anyway? The creep never bothered much with his son during her brother's short life. It was Grace, and Grace alone, who had really cared for Liam. Grace who stayed home with the boy after she finished high school, taking early morning health and social science courses so that her mother could work afternoons and nights. Grace who played with him, fed him, put him down for his nap, bathed him, dressed him, wiped the cracker crumbs from his sweet, puckered mouth. Old friends from school came and went, got jobs or attended the local community college, slowly disappearing from her life while her little brother took center stage, the siblings so close to one another that her mother joked they should have been twins.

Liam had red curly hair, much like Grace's, and he loved animals, particularly fish and mice. He liked to draw and to sip pudding through a straw.

He was trying to catch a squirrel when he was hit by a car.

She had let go of his hand. It was only for a moment—she turned and looked the other way and his warm fingers had slipped from her own.

They never found the driver. Hit and run, the police told her. A terrible crime with terrible consequences. They would certainly find Liam's killer. They would not rest until this was achieved. They promised her mother that.

Grace pulls out the sweater from the suitcase and sits down. The mattress feels thin and hard. She's tired. She'll stop thinking about all of this. She promised herself. Remembering has done her no good at all.

The small oval mirror, balanced precariously on the bureau top, falls over suddenly with the sound of a slap, and when Grace steadies it, she notices the surface is cracked. She stares at herself in the fragmented pieces, her face divided by uneven shards of glass, and can't help but smirk at her distorted reflection. Her wild mop of auburn hair colors her face with a copperish tint, giving the impression of another's glowing shadow hovering closely behind. Her wide freckled nose is chopped in two, her brown, heavy-lidded eyes are suddenly lopsided, and her full mouth is divided in half, one side hanging down in a solemn frown and the other upturned, as if in evil delight. The oval scar on the left side of her lower lip, from the time she burned herself while blowing out birthday candles, multiplies in the shattered glass. Eight years old, and the last birthday celebration she can remember. After that year, a clumsily wrapped present would appear on the breakfast table with a note: *Happy birthday, Gracie. Back by ten. Remember to take out the trash—Mom*

She laughs hoarsely, looking into the shattered mirror again, a bitter taste filling her mouth. It's a miracle, and really difficult to understand, how such a small, damaged sliver of glass could capture her entire fleshy, bloated face.

． ． ．

When Grace finally opens her bedroom door, she's overwhelmed by the house's silence. Of course the grandmother's room is quiet, as is to be expected—Grace will check inside later in the day to see what needs to be done—but the boy's door is slightly ajar, yet she can't hear any sign of life. When she knocks, she's surprised by his invitation to enter, and then not surprised when he still refuses to look at her or say much of anything.

She offers him dinner but he seems hesitant, and it's no wonder he's so thin, claiming that he hardly eats an evening meal at all. He's clearly a boy who needs some real nourishment, and it will probably be a challenge to get him to eat. Sometimes you just have to take it slowly with kids—Grace somehow knows that she can't rush it, and that, for a while anyway, she'll have to adapt to his pace.

Even so, she goes downstairs to the kitchen in order to prepare dinner. Whether he's up to joining her or not, she is not going to forget to eat, for her own pleasure and to keep up her strength. Although Grace made breakfast that very morning, she didn't have time to thoroughly explore the kitchen, and now, when she opens the large varnished cabinet door, to her surprise and alarm, the shelves are almost completely empty: there's hardly any food at all. She peers at the shelf above the oven and sees a small pot of "bouquet garni" and a blue box of "sel de mer," and wonders what on earth these labels mean. A large tin of Irish oatmeal glitters ferociously in a dark corner of the next cabinet, but nothing more. She closes the door and opens another directly to the right of the sink. Two cans of sardines, and one of smoked mussels. Smoked mussels? Who in the world would want to eat that? Melba toast is piled neatly in an oblong plastic container and three kinds of specialty teas—chamomile, peach, and raspberry—are sealed in plastic wrap.

No wonder the boy's starving.

A cabinet in the corner contains a little more. Six small cans of tuna packed in spring water—that might be useful in a casserole. A cellophane bag of whole-wheat pasta, two jars of plum tomatoes, and a single container of sundried tomatoes.

Things were looking up.

She opens the refrigerator gingerly, knowing already that it's half empty. Thank god for the small carton of Egg Beaters, a half quart of orange juice, and another of skim milk. A small bowl is covered with tinfoil neatly crimped around the edges like a piecrust, and she peers underneath to find baby greens topped with three tiny cherry tomatoes. No dressing to be found. The butter and egg trays are empty, the meat drawer spotted with bits of yellow cheese. The package must have slipped open: "lite cheddar." Of course.

Inside the vegetable bin she finds a stalk of celery and a bag of baby carrots. Directly beneath is another container, for fruit. Two pink grapefruits, two lemons, four limes, a single blood orange. Nothing else. The interior of the freezer door is covered with frost, as is a half-eaten bag of broccoli. There are five packages of Lean Cuisine, four chicken and one vegetable.

Well, she's certainly not going to bother with any of that. How did these two survive in such a deprived household, and how is she supposed to feed a growing boy as well as herself?

Of course, it's been a long while since Grace has done much real cooking, usually satisfied with fast food and packaged snacks and desserts. Too much trouble to make full-fledged meals, and much easier to fill her kitchen at home with convenient treats. Grace's mother hardly eats at the apartment anyway, taking her meals at the restaurant. But now, Grace has someone else to think about, a child, someone in real need of support and help.

Tomorrow morning, if the boy's up to staying at home alone, she'll go shopping for fresh groceries. For now, she opens the bag of bowtie pasta, then roots around the bottom cabinet shelves for pots and pans. Two kettles are lined up side by side, one small, as if for boiling water for coffee, and the other larger. The rest of the shelf is completely empty. She fills the large one with tap water and sets it on the stove to heat. She'll cook the pasta and then use a jar of plum tomatoes as a sauce. Maybe the bits of cheese can be used as a garnish, and maybe the scent of her cooking will tempt the boy to come downstairs, but for now she's too exhausted to even care.

She finds herself wishing desperately for a chocolate bar, a sandwich cookie filled with dark fudge, a wedge of buttercream layer cake, a peppermint or lemon drop, something sweet to suck on, for goodness' sake, anything at all. But this is a barren house, empty of everything but the most basic necessities. There's barely anything to eat at all.

It's been a long and difficult day. She sits down on the white wooden chair and for a moment worries that it will crack under her weight. But it doesn't; the legs hold firm. She waits for the water to bubble, listens to her stomach growl and rumble, then watches for the empty, windowless room to fill up with fog and smoke.

· DAY TWO ·

GRACE

It's 7:00 A.M. when Grace awakens, and the house is perfectly quiet. She dresses quickly, finding a pair of navy sweatpants and a hooded sweater to match. No point in formality, and she must wear something warm despite the late summer month since the house is kept surprisingly cool, in fact, freezing—she hasn't been able to find the air-conditioning thermostat and found herself shivering in the middle of the night, without an extra blanket anywhere to provide warmth.

The small bathroom down the hall is between the boy's room and the grandmother's room, so she decides to shower later in the evening, worried about disturbing the household so early in the day. A good sleep is important for all after such a difficult time. Oh, well, Grace thinks, she should be able to get to the store and back before breakfast. Last night she made a list of groceries and looks for it in the pocket of her sweater. Grace wishes she had her favorite red baseball cap, the one she can wear in all seasons, the one that covers her thick, unruly hair, but unfortunately she lost it somewhere several weeks ago.

Before leaving, she hesitates, listening carefully in the upstairs hallway just in case she's needed. But there's nothing, not even the faintest stirring, so Grace takes a deep breath, walks quietly downstairs, and opens the front door.

Although it's summer, the morning air's brisk. She drove by a corner grocery the other afternoon and knows it's just a few blocks away, so she decides to walk. The streets are empty, but to her surprise, there's a small crowd of women gathering outside the shop door. They look up as she walks by, making her uncomfortable, although the feeling quickly passes. She has a job to do and it must be accomplished swiftly in order to get back to the house as soon as she can.

She'll be needed there.

By the time Grace finishes, her cart is filled with fresh produce, a boxed chocolate cake, two cartons of eggs, butter, flour, sliced cheddar cheese, three bags of cookies—shortbread, chocolate chip and sugar wafer—a loaf of soft potato bread, bacon, two steaks, a pound of ground beef, and even more. She worries that she won't be able to carry it all home by herself and considers returning with the car. But at the last minute she changes her mind and balances a bag on each arm, the last one slung over her wrist, and clutches a cinnamon bun in one hand to eat on the way home. She feels it stick to her palm, the walnuts piercing her skin, and imagines how the buttery carmel topping will melt on her tongue during the walk back to the small house. As Grace leaves the store, she glances over at the counter where a pile of newspapers are being examined by two women, hoping that no one will notice the trail of sugary crumbs left behind.

"Unbelievable," one says to the other. "He was just in here yesterday. I saw him myself." "Do they have any clues?"

The taller woman looks pale, shaken, like she might keel right over in a dead faint.

The conversation stops suddenly, and, curious, Grace bends over to read the paper's headline as she opens the shop door, wishing she had read the entire paper before.

Prominent Doctor Murdered
in Suburban Home
One Shot to the Heart

The bun is disintegrating in her hand.

The grocery bags' plastic handles dig into her skin like teeth.

Grace shivers and, arms aching, walks quickly back to the little brick house.

"We don't eat egg yolks and certainly not bacon. Mademoiselle says animal fat will kill you."

Grace looks up from her cooking to see the boy standing in his usual hunched position at the kitchen door.

"Good morning," she says, ignoring his comment. "Come sit down and have something to eat. Kids your age have to be fed a good breakfast. You know, the most important meal of the day."

She slides two fried eggs and three slices of bacon onto a plate. She can feel him watching, as if she has just committed a terrible crime.

"I don't mean to be impolite"—he is standing perfectly still, in place—"but I thought I just made mention of the fact that we do not eat certain foods."

"All right, then." Grace finds herself feeling surprisingly irritated. This is just the first day. The boy's had to adjust to many changes in his life over the past twenty-four hours and she knows she must give him a chance. And she can see that he's not ready to face the facts of his grandmother's sudden absence and that she, Noah's temporary caretaker, must tread gently, at least for a while. "Just sit down and we'll figure out something else for you to eat."

"You are here to take care of the household," she hears him murmur as he slides, head down as usual, onto the kitchen chair. "I do not need a babysitter. I am perfectly able to tend to myself."

"Are you?" She butters two pieces of bread. "Then tell me, how you are planning to feed yourself this morning so that you stay healthy? What can I make for you? After all, it's you who needs a hearty breakfast, not your grandmother."

Complete silence. Grace is immediately ashamed of herself and bites her lip. How could she have said something so incredibly stupid?

Finally he exhales a little sigh and squeezes his hands together as if praying.

"Sometimes," he says evenly, in a voice suddenly much older than his years and bigger than his size, "sometimes we will eat oatmeal in the morning. Sometimes we will eat fruit."

"Good."

She reaches for the cabinet where she saw the tin of oatmeal the night before, but just as she tries to pull it down, he suddenly springs to her side.

"Don't. I'll do it."

She can hear him breathing quickly, and realizes this is as close to her as he has stood. She can even feel his dry breath on her neck and her heart lurches.

She notices that he's wearing the same clothes as the day before, a starched light blue oxford shirt stiffly buttoned up to his chin and neatly tucked into immaculate, crisply pressed khaki trousers. Grace wonders how the pleat in his pants can stay so perfectly creased, flattened into a solid seam, looking more like cardboard than fabric. Is it her imagination, or does Noah walk without bending his knees, more like a robot or puppet instead of a real human boy?

And earlier that day, Grace had discovered that the grandmother also had a peculiar way of dressing, although entirely different from her grandson. Where Noah was conservative and subdued, the old woman appeared to favor extravagant clothing, kind of flashy and hardly appropriate for a woman of her age. That very morning, when Grace was leaving for the store, she had checked the hallway closet for an umbrella because it looked like rain. When the door swung open, the light blazed on automatically, as if powered by an invisible hand, and she quickly stepped back, overcome with an odor she found difficult to identify. Grace inhaled, then coughed. The interior was musty, clearly sealed off for a long while, and her nose was filled with sudden bitterness, cloying and unpleasant at the same time. A mixture of mothballs, mold, and rot—and something else as well. A scent that reminded her of whisky or cognac, acidic and still a little sweet.

Despite the smell, the closet was immaculate, everything clearly in its place, a row of four women's hats lined up neatly on the shelf above: the first scarlet, broad brimmed and feathered, the left side pinned up with a cut-glass amber brooch. Next, a fedora covered with a leopard print, the fuzzy material a poor imitation of animal skin, yet somehow still convincingly real. Then a pink felt pillbox smothered with purple netting, tiny rhinestones lining the fragile veil's rim; and, finally, a small red beret, evidently too soft to stand at attention all on its own like its companions, but crumpled flat into a small circle, a child's deflated balloon.

The coats hanging below were similarly positioned, also arranged in a perfect row, each an equal distance from the other: a fur stole of some kind, only partially visible and stuffed into a long transparent storage bag; a short white leather jacket with a crimson silk scarf tucked into one pocket like a severed hand; a navy trench coat cinched so tightly at the waist that it resembled someone punched smack in the stomach and curled over in distress; and, finally, a black satin cape, sinuously wound around its hanger's soft, pink padded neck.

Four purses swung from a silver hook on the back of the door, grazing Grace's head and making her spin around in alarm. She was struck by their size, each tinier than the next, the first intricately beaded with a red fringe and glittering clasp; the next shiny black leather, triangular and capped with sharp metal at the corners; the third a soft flesh-colored pouch, sagging from its enormous pearl clasp like a wrinkled throat. The entire collection gave the impression of belonging to a dwarf or a gnome, to someone or something extraordinarily small. Grace found it hard to imagine any of these items being carried by a human, someone made of real flesh and blood.

Sitting across from Noah at the formica

kitchen table, Grace looks down at her palms, her hands enormous, ruddy, padded with flesh, each one larger than a single one of those little purses, and once again feels like a giant lumbering through the tiny world of a miniature race.

"I'll do it. I'll make oatmeal for us both," she hears Noah repeat, and she looks up suddenly, as if awakened from a dream. "But I can tell you that my grandmother never eats more than a tablespoon or two each morning, accompanied by a tepid cup of Earl Gray or English Breakfast tea."

Startled by the boy's odd remark, Grace doesn't say anything, but sits down in front of the warm eggs and bacon and lifts her fork. The old woman may have taught the boy to be satisfied with tiny bites of cold oatmeal; he may feel comfortable being all sinew and bone, covered in starched clothing, nothing but a stiff frame; but Grace is determined to work on filling him out and loosening him up—after all, this is an important part of her work. For now, however, she'll make sure to take care of her own needs, her own pleasure and nourishment.

This good food lined up in front of her will

certainly not go to waste, and her mouth waters in anticipation. Grace watches Noah's thin back bend over the counter and suddenly wonders what he means by making oatmeal for "us both." His grandmother certainly wouldn't be having any breakfast, and she herself has no intention of touching the slimy, tasteless stuff.

Noah and Grace sit on the long cream living room couch, the only piece of furniture in the entire room, with the exception of a glass coffee table, two small empty white china bowls in the exact center. Grace can easily picture this couch smothered in a plastic cover—in fact, she suddenly realizes that it's easy to imagine this whole house wrapped, sealed up, preserved, untouched by human hands.

She sits at one end and the boy at the other. She thinks of the cookies in the kitchen across the hall, nestled neatly in layers of crisply pleated white paper cups, each one snuggled safely in place. She wonders which she will devour first.

They're reading the newspaper.

Grace notices Noah delicately licking his index finger before turning each page. She's pleased that he's sitting with her in the same room. She wonders if she should broach the topic of the grandmother, but thinks better of it. At least for now.

"Do you know where North Street is?" she asks, skimming through the article about the local murder. "I'm not familiar with this neighborhood."

"Why?" He looks up quickly, as if alarmed, and then hangs his head again so as not to meet her gaze.

"No reason, nothing in particular." Somehow she's hesitant to share the details of the crime, him being so young and going through such a difficult time.

"No, really, I want to know." He almost looks right at her and she is encouraged by the eye contact.

"It's nothing important, at least not to us, but there seems to have been an incident over on North Street. Number 1205."

"What kind of incident?"

"An unfortunate assault, a shooting. The details are vague. Wouldn't you like to read the comics? I think I saw some underneath this page."

Grace feels uncomfortable discussing the murder with the boy. She doesn't want to take the chance of upsetting him or causing him any more anxiety than is necessary.

She knows what can happen.

How horror can suddenly smack you in the face.

Grace realizes that she is squeezing her hands so tightly together that her fingernails are digging into her skin, and idly wonders if it's too early in the morning to offer the boy a slice of lemon cake for a snack. Suddenly she's starving, as if breakfast had been eaten hours ago. It isn't normal for a grown woman to hunger from morning to night, to never be satisfied even when full, to never ever have enough. Grace knows this, and yet . . .

Noah is staring at her intently, even paler than ever, his lips moving slightly, almost imperceptibly, but without words. Has she upset him with the news of the crime? Grace changes the subject again and tries to get him to talk to her, to open up and confide. She'd like to know about his past, his friends, his school, the details of his life. And she knows that it's very important for him to talk about his grandmother and the confusing emotions he must have. But she quickly realizes that she has calculated incorrectly, pushed too fast, too far.

By the time it's clear that Grace is making Noah uncomfortable with her probing, it's already too late. She watches as he draws back as if cornered. She notices the impatient tapping of his foot. She holds her breath and anticipates his departure.

She's silent as he leaves the room.

Grace leans back on the couch, suddenly exhausted, and listens for his door to slam, but instead hears nothing at all.

She remembers how hungry she is and thinks of the sweets purchased earlier. Although tired, she'll stand and hurry to the kitchen. She'll fill herself until there is nothing to want anymore.

· DAY THREE ·

NOAH

The news of the shooting consumes me.

And once I apologize to Nurse Grace for my rudeness, once I explain that I am simply upset about Mademoiselle, and my impolite behavior had nothing to do with the news of the crime at all, she completely relents.

"Why don't we take a minute to talk about your grandmother," she adds suddenly. "I know that you must have a lot on your mind."

"I prefer not to discuss that particular subject," I respond crossly, and then try to smile quickly again. The last thing I want is Nurse Grace attempting to use psychology and thinking I am avoiding what must be said.

Next, I am able to successfully convince this stranger that my curiosity about the recent murder is the result of its proximity, which is partly the truth. After all, North Street is next to my junior high school, only five blocks away. This seems to appease Nurse Grace's concerns that any information regarding the murder will traumatize me, that I am somehow not old or strong enough to know the plain facts of life, and I am thus able to freely scour the newspapers and listen to the radio, without her irritating intervention.

In fact, oddly enough, Nurse Grace becomes interested in the shooting as well, perhaps figuring our common focus will bond us in some unimaginable way. It is strange how she seems so intent on getting to know me as this is really not her job here, and why would she bother with a thirteen-year-old boy at all? I chalk it up to her own loneliness; it is quite clear that she is a woman without many friends or family, and I find it pathetic that a full-grown adult cannot occupy herself without the company of someone almost half her age.

Somehow, I suddenly think of my grandmother and how she knew it was best to leave me to myself. While we did have our moments together, she let me have privacy and protected her own. And at this moment, I am tempted to rush up to her bedroom door, compelled to peek my head inside and quietly call out her name. But I know that this would be foolhardy, really no point to such an exercise at all, as my poor Mademoiselle would not be able to respond. I think of her and suddenly miss her company intensely. But I will not think of this, I will try not to remember the surgery and my grandmother's pain.

I certainly have my hands full with the intrepid Nurse Grace and notice that she has not received a visit or personal phone call during the time spent at our house, and I never hear her talking about a boyfriend or her family. In fact, I don't hear her say much about herself at all. There have been a number of other phone calls that she has made, but they most definitely were of the professional bent.

On several occasions I have overheard Nurse Grace speaking softly in the next room. I'm not exactly eavesdropping, since this is my house, after all. I listen to her murmuring about "healing" and "progress," and know that she is probably conferring with her supervisor or someone else working on this case. I hope she knows what she is doing, that she has been adequately trained for a job such as this.

After all, not just anyone can deal with someone else's suffering; it takes a particularly educated mind and an extremely gentle hand. It was not my position to check her references before the operation, and I hope that this process was a thorough one, that she is both skilled and understanding.

Nurse Grace clearly seems to try very hard, but I am not convinced that she is efficient and well organized, or that she knows how to deal effectively with those in pain, with the infirm.

Helping someone to heal takes talent. It is a question not only of science, but of compassion.

How do I know this? I am not actually quite sure.

When Nurse Grace returns from her trip to the store this morning, we both crowd around the kitchen table, spreading the newspaper in front of us so we can read at the same time. She unpacks a round coffee cake wrapped in cellophane, a large bunch of bananas, a pint of strawberries, a package of vanilla wafer cookies, and a box of instant hot chocolate. I wonder where all the food will fit in our small tidy kitchen and begin to feel sick to my stomach.

"Hungry?"

She smiles and rips off the cake's cellophane in one motion.

I ignore her question and turn back to the newspaper. The details about the murder continue to be unnerving, as the assailant remains at large, the only eyewitness repeating the original account of seeing a young boy.

"Hmm," Nurse Grace says as she drops crumbs of coffee cake on the paper. "It seems that someone would have noticed something more. The murder was committed in broad daylight, in the late afternoon. Did you read anything about the doctor being alone in the house, or was someone else there?"

"What doctor?" I am trying to ignore the loose pieces of cake that have dropped from her fork and that cover every other printed word; I wonder exactly what the taste might be, such a peculiar color, too light a brown to be chocolate and definitely too dark to be anything else. But what kind of adult would eat chocolate cake for breakfast? That seems quite odd, even for Nurse Grace.

The crumb topping falls onto the paper in large, irregular clumps. This is not a proper way to eat a meal.

"You know, the doctor who was shot."

"I didn't know he was a doctor."

"Yes, a surgeon—it says so right here, and look, he was alone. Apparently his wife was out of town and the poor man was minding his own business, watching television with a glass of wine in his hand." She clucks her tongue softly. "What a shame. A man like that, one who has probably helped so many, shot down in his prime. I wonder what the motive was? There must be more to this than anyone knows."

I feel my throat tighten. Nurse Grace tries to examine my face, but I have hidden it behind one hand.

"Are you all right, Noah? You haven't finished your breakfast."

I study the grapefruit half on my plate and push it away.

"Not hungry," I respond.

Why is food always the center of any discussion between us, why is it important at all?

"But we talked about this yesterday. You've got to eat something." She cuts a small slice of cake and puts it on the side of my plate. "Why don't you taste the coffee cake? It's fresh, just bought from the store."

I shake my head but am surprised to hear my voice ask out loud, "What kind is it, anyway? I certainly do not want any, but wonder what variety it might be."

She smiles, I think a bit smugly, then takes an enormous bite.

"Cinnamon," she answers, her mouth half full, so I can barely understand her muffled words. "Cinnamon, my absolute favorite."

Is it my imagination or do I feel my mouth begin to water? Is that my own stomach rumbling, a foreign, unfamiliar sound? But then I remember the murder, and begin to feel sick all over again.

●   ●   ●

Later, in the afternoon, I manage to find some time to spend by myself in my room. It seems more and more difficult to acquire any privacy, a situation entirely unfamiliar and disquieting for someone of my temperament and my needs. While Mademoiselle and I have had some very interesting chats during my years growing up in this small house, she was always more comfortable keeping to herself and letting me keep to mine.

My grandmother was not a very social or active woman, although, as noted before, she had the finest of manners and the most exquisite of taste. She preferred to be alone in her room most of the day, resting, reading magazines like *Variety*, or the romance novels I would buy for her at the corner store. She also loved watching television and would often keep it on from morning to night. Sometimes, in the early evening, after I brought her a glass of sherry, we would watch *Wheel of Fortune* together, me sitting Indian style on the floor next to her bed, and her half reclining, half leaning forward, sipping sherry delicately, sometimes asking for more. We kept a leaded decanter filled to the brim on her bedstand, in case she needed a refill in the middle of the night.

"It helps me sleep, my darling," she would say, and smile, sometimes holding the glass up in front of her like a prism, the crystal chandelier above reflected in the etched triangular corners of frozen light. Then she would close her eyes, the empty glass still clutched in her hand, and ask me for just a little bit more. "Thank you, my dear," she would murmur, as I carefully poured the thick amber. "Just leave the rest right by my side in case I need something to help me sleep during the long night."

And I did just as I was asked, setting down the goblet on a fleur-de-lis doily and pulling her silk covers right up to her chin. Sometimes her hair would be rolled and wrapped in ordinary white toilet paper. "An old beauty trick from my vaudeville days," she once told me. "It keeps your hairdo perfectly in place." Sometimes her face would be covered in an aloe mask, project-ing a most peculiar greenish glow, making her look both scary and sweet at the very same time, a little ghoulish elf, a diminutive forest troll.

But, always, she would eventually slip on her white satin eye mask, and then I would know it was time for me to go.

While in my room, and having escaped from Nurse Grace, I suddenly find myself drawn to my closet, where I keep a half-full scrapbook and my secret box. Of course, Mademoiselle knew about the scrapbook, and even added to it with a few clippings of her own. During our younger years, we used to sit on her bed together and cut out articles from a collection of old newspapers and magazines, then press down with slim white glue sticks so that every corner would adhere.

CONJOINED TWINS BORN IN CHILDREN'S HOSPITAL was the headline of our town paper dated April 1, 1989, and the subtitle read: *Doctors Have Little Hope of Babies' Survival.*

"Such crude language," Mademoiselle would often say, clucking her tongue and shaking her head. "You would think that professional writers might express themselves in a more refined manner. And I'm certainly glad that those reporters never got wind of what the priest said the night of your birth. Why, he was completely baffled, my dear, and didn't know what to do. He couldn't quite assess how many souls inhabited your twin bodies, exactly who was to be baptized or how many sacraments were required. A bit humorous, when you think about it."

Then she laughed.

I think of this as I reach for my scrapbook and open it to the first page. Were we born with double souls or with individual spirits of our own?

It has been a long time since I pulled the collection of papers and photographs out of hiding, and I look carefully at a yellowing Polaroid of a young woman holding a dark bundle in her arms. It is impossible to see either her face or the babies', and the corners of the picture are darkening with age. An odd yellow substance seeps from the photograph, probably some kind of chemical, and the picture emanates a pungent odor, like a mixture of paste and perfume. I inhale it greedily, somehow comforted by the scent, both familiar and noxious. I bend my head in an effort to more carefully study the picture, but the closer I get, the more the fumes make me feel ill.

I turn the page. Next is *The Petersburgh Gazette* column about our birth in Children's Hospital, the one to which Mademoiselle so objected, the article indicating little chance of survival. It includes a photograph of a doctor with one of those silly caps worn during surgery and a wide smile on his face. The article itself is short, dwarfed by the headline and the photograph; there is little room for actual text. The following page includes a paragraph from *Time* magazine, simply giving the facts surrounding the birth. No prognosis is noted.

I sigh.

I usually skip the next few pages, although Mademoiselle insisted on including them despite my request that they be destroyed. It feels unseemly to keep these particular publications forever, available for anyone to see, glued permanently to this large, bound canvas book. Why would I want to preserve information about the actual surgery, about my own brother's untimely death? I close the book suddenly, and reach under the closet floorboards for my box, so completely hidden that even Mademoiselle never knew it was there.

No one knows, and no one ever will know.

This is the Private Box of the Invisible Boy, and while I'm not quite sure why I keep it, I'm also certain that if it were found, no one would ever understand. The container itself is smaller than a jewelry box, really no larger than a child's hand. It is blue, made of porcelain, and was probably once used for pills or something of the kind. Once I manage to pull it out from underneath the wood flooring and make sure tape still holds the lid firmly in place, once I am certain it is sealed permanently and no one has peered inside, I always return the small carton to its narrow grave and push the floorboard nails back as far as they can possibly go.

I sit at the bottom of my bedroom closet, wedged in between a pair of leather dress shoes and the scrapbook that chronicles my birth and my twin brother's death. A small black suit from my childhood, made of the finest imported wool, swings above me, the hem of its trousers skimming the top of my head.

I shiver.

The floor of my small closet is cold and there is no room for me to spread my arms or legs. I hear something, the floor or the roof, creaking from below and then from above and I wrap my arms around myself. Probably just the wind sneaking into the house's crevices, and I suddenly think of Mademoiselle's eerie whistling as she sleeps. I feel my legs begin to tingle and then suddenly realize that they are both immobile, rigid; without my knowing, my limbs have fallen dead asleep.

I lean back and wait; it will be a while before I am able to stand up again without the offer of someone else's strength.

· DAY FOUR ·

NOAH

The next morning I rush downstairs to read the newspaper, but Nurse Grace has beaten me to it. She sits at the kitchen table, the paper spread out before her, eating pancakes covered with strawberry jam.

"Strawberry jam?" I try to peer over her shoulder. "Why jam on pancakes? I have certainly never heard of that."

"Why not?" She turns and smiles up at me before I have time to look the other way. I still choose not to look directly into this woman's huge face. "Good morning, Noah. Sit down here. I've made something even you won't be able to resist."

I slide myself onto a chair. I am hesitant at best.

In a small cut-crystal bowl before me is a

collection of quivering colors, a melange of every possible seasonal fruit: grapes, watermelon, cantaloupe, blackberries, blueberries, and even bananas, each cut up into tiny pieces, almost in slivers, as if made for a baby's little mouth. The fruit glistens, quivering with different hues—green, red, orange, yellow, dark purple, and blue—and flecked with what looks like the most delicate of snowflakes. White curlicues—sugar, either confectioners' or refined.

"Thank you very much," I say slowly. "I appreciate the effort, but you know I prefer not to eat white sugar. Even the smallest amount is harmful to my heart."

Nurse Grace just grins and pushes the bowl to me. The fruit jiggles as if shivering, then settles into its luminous nest.

"Coconut," she chortles. "I found shredded coconut at the store. It's unsweetened. Here, try some."

She leans over as if to feed me, and that is when I have had enough.

"Please," I say carefully, making certain not to be rude. "I think, at my age, I should be able to manage all by myself."

I pick up my spoon tentatively.

"Must you stare at me so intently?" I ask. "I think it's poor form to watch someone as they are trying to have a meal."

She nods, then picks up the newspaper with both hands.

I dip my spoon into the bowl and hear it clatter, then slide it slowly into my mouth, its cold metal warming quickly to my tongue.

The fruit is both acidic and sweet, a collection of flavors I have never quite tasted before, and the coconut studs each bite with a chewy texture. I swallow and then swallow again. My mouth tingles, then my throat, then all the way down. My stomach, usually empty, scoured clean through and through, is suddenly filled with skin and juices, even tiny particles of forgotten seed and membrane. I eat faster and faster and try to imagine my intestines, the twisted route the food follows, and where it settles, staying right there all the way inside. Do the fragments simply float together, or do they layer themselves to form another whole?

I feel myself expanding and then making room for even more.

Nurse Grace's face remains covered by the newspaper, but I can imagine her smiling from ear to ear.

"Ambrosia," she eventually says softly. "You're eating ambrosia, which means 'food of the gods.'"

I don't say anything, my mouth full at the time, but Mademoiselle and I do not believe in deities or the afterlife.

We have enough trouble with the here and now.

After we are finished eating, Nurse Grace puts down the paper, shakes her head, and hands me the front page.

Another shooting, another murder. Again near this very house.

This time by the town cinema, just a few blocks away. A man filling up his car at a neighborhood gas station was shot right in the head.

Once more, nobody saw the shooter. No one saw a car leaving the scene or anyone running away. The whole town is under siege, terrified—at least that's what Nurse Grace tells me the paper says.

The murderer has left a message this time, she informs me. Not a note or letter, but, of all things, the tarot Card of Death.

The police found the card near the scene, across the street from the crime, and have determined that the bullet is from a sniper rifle, and that the murderer has extensive experience with guns. Maybe someone from the military, maybe someone with police training, maybe a traitor with connections to another government, maybe even one of them.

The paper is full of it. And a photograph of the card is included: a picture of a small skeleton lying on the ground among fallen, curled leaves. A long snake, maybe a cobra, surrounds the bones and two white tree trunks that look like birch are rooted firmly in the ground.

"From the Major Arcana series," Nurse Grace tells me. "The tarot deck's divided into two sections, Major and Minor Arcana. The Death Card is from the Major Arcana—quite a strange choice, since this part of the deck is known for universal truths. While the Minor Arcana section speaks to the ordinary things of life, the Major reveals life's greater secrets and spiritual meaning."

"What exactly are tarot cards, anyway?" As usual, the house is cold and I try to warm the goose bumps on my arms by rubbing them with both hands.

"Oh, it's quite interesting. I used to experiment with the tarot deck as a girl. You know, we'd all have silly seances with lit candles and the like."

I find it difficult to imagine Nurse Grace as a young girl. She is double the height and triple the width of any girl I have ever seen. As of yet, I have not even looked into her face, but usually try to address her by staring at her ample waist. Lately, however, I have worked my way up a bit. Starting with looking at her feet the first day she arrived, then scanning up to her middle, I now find my eyes concentrated on her neck. She is wearing a yellow shirt with a round collar, and I can see a bit of double chin wobble each time she speaks.

"Tarot's ages old," she continues, standing up to clear our plates. "I'm not really sure when the practice started, but sometime way, way before either of us, even before our grandparents' grandparents were born. Maybe as far back as, geez, I don't know—but a long, long time ago. The deck's often used for meditation and predicting the future, you know, to both relax and get in touch with your own feelings—that kind of thing. Some folks really believe that the cards can tell you what's going to happen; and some others, including an old aunt of mine, think that tarot can actually can help you develop a sixth sense—you know, like ESP. My aunt told me, however, that although the cards really don't predict much of anything, they can help you understand yourself as you are. The pictures and figures shown are meant to get you to focus on thoughts about people and situations in your own life. Each of the cards can be read differently, and mean something different, at different times to different people, but tarot usually has something to do with learning about yourself. Some of the cards are actually quite difficult to interpret and understand."

"Well, this one is already clear," I say, pointing to the photograph in the paper. "It doesn't seem as though there is much room for different interpretations for death."

"Oh, I'm not so sure."

Nurse Grace is sponging off the kitchen table, and I wish she would reconsider and use a paper towel instead. Sponges are breeding grounds for bacteria—Mademoiselle's permanent instructions were never to contaminate one's home in such a thoughtless way.

"Actually, if I remember correctly, the Death Card is not all it seems. Most think of it as the obvious, but my understanding is that it is more complicated than this. The skeleton seen here"— she points to the newspaper—"doesn't only indicate death but also completion and change. It represents a cycle, something that's coming to a close, allowing one to move on."

Ha, I think, slowly standing up. I certainly doubt that the murderer, this assassin in our midst, is concerned with personal evolution or transformation of any kind. I yawn; my stomach suddenly feels pleasantly full and I am oddly sleepy. Death is clearly as permanent as it gets, I muse, thoroughly unconvinced that the creator of the delicate drawing on the murderer's card meant this skeleton to go anywhere but into the hard cold ground.

That afternoon, having escaped from Nurse Grace's clutches for a while, I lie on my bed and study the rows of books on each wall.

I feel almost fortunate.

Ever since I can remember, I have been lured by the written word, captivated and entranced.

Thank goodness for the company of books, for the comfort they bring. When there is no one with whom to talk, their pages invite you to wander inside, and when your own life rejects you, enticing characters open their arms.

I am grateful for my small library, which I recently learned belonged to my father a very long time ago. Apparently he was an avid reader and a collector of literature, like me, but Mademoiselle once told me he was also a failed author, and that he had absolutely no talent of any kind.

"Just a shame, just a tragedy that he took your mother with him when he died. He may have been my own son, this much is true; but, my dear, we never really got along well, even when he was just a small boy."

She stared into her dressing table mirror for a moment as if hoping for a surprise, then spun around to face me, thick black liner framing her small eyes.

"So insolent, so rude, never took no for an answer, never really learned to behave properly as a child. He was strong-headed and stubborn, with a temperament quite different from mine. Sometimes, when he was small, I thought I might go crazy chasing him about the house. A woman of my caliber is used to proper respect from everyone, particularly her own flesh and blood."

She inhaled sharply and then went on as though talking to herself.

"Of course, I always cared for him a great deal—after all, he was my only son—but I never understood his ways, and the accident soon ended any possibility of that."

Mademoiselle sighed and dabbed her face

with a cotton ball, then continued talking, looking past me to address the wall.

"You know it was he who was driving, and he had been drinking that night. I hate to admit it, my darling, but your father was quite a lush. There's nothing wrong with enjoying oneself—I certainly have no problem with that—but one must use discretion, absolutely never indulge in public at all. And the crash so unnecessary—if only she had been behind the wheel. But there was no convincing him of anything once he had made up his mind, once he was decided, always so sure of himself, always adamant.

"Of course, I knew nothing of it until the police finally called. I'm certainly glad that I wasn't there to see as their bodies were hauled out of that godforsaken car."

How I longed to ask her a myriad of questions then—was my mother beautiful, my father strong and brave? Their photographs had once lined our mantelpiece, but my grandmother had long ago put them away. I knew better than to ask her to let me see them, and my parents' faces soon began to fade from my mind. Did they love each other? I would wonder. What did they like to eat, where did they shop, what were their favorite places to visit, special traditions between them, beloved books; how much did they care for me, want me, mourn my other. How sad were they when he died, how bereaved when he was lost, how lonesome?

But I knew better. I knew to close my mouth until all of my questions melted on my sliver of a tongue. I knew not to say a word.

My grandmother turned quickly back to the dressing table, a grimace on her face, and then began gathering hairpins from a drawer, examining them intently, as if each one were alive. She stiffened for a moment, then slowly shook her head, suddenly twisting her hair into tight circles and stabbing them with the hairpins one by one.

I recognized this ritual, as she repeated it most every night. She was preparing her hair for styling in the morning, although she rarely went out of the house. It was painful to watch as she pulled brutally at her exposed scalp. It shone in between the rows of the pin curls, like varnished white flesh. I was always reminded of natives deep in the jungle as they decorated themselves for war, applying face paint thoroughly and piercing their own flesh. Some thought them savage but I knew better than that.

I remember feeling sickened but determined not to cry. Mademoiselle drew her robe around her and then started slowly for the bed.

The windows were completely concealed with heavy beige brocade that swayed slowly as if someone was breathing fitfully from inside. My grandmother reached out her hand toward me, but then drew it back again. I remember being disappointed, and then relieved after all.

I think Mademoiselle suddenly noticed that I was seated much too far away.

I think she remembered how much she hated to be touched.

The sunlight suddenly streams through my window, illuminating each and every one of my books and swarming each title with a hazy glow. Then the letters themselves shimmer, flickering like birthday candles under a child's pursed lips. Their spines, some wide, some narrow, seem to breathe in and out, and magically change size and shape as if touched by a magician's wand.

A single book instead of many.

Only one that holds the key?

Exactly which might that be?

Why did my father insist on driving, and what did he say to my mother that night? Perhaps they were planning my future, how I might be educated, where I would live, what college to attend. Maybe he turned up the radio, maybe he reached for her hand. She might have smiled at him warmly. She might have blown him a kiss.

Their heads could have fused for a moment, one instead of two. Their last minutes could have been loving, my name on both their lips.

I close my eyes for a minute and then open them quickly again. There is an enormous text on the top bookshelf on the opposite wall. Huge yet barely visible it lies down in the shadow, so I can hardly make out its name. In fact, I cannot remember ever noticing such an enormous, majestic tome before.

For some reason it is difficult to stand, to

walk across the room. I feel unusually tired, perhaps coming down with a cold or flu. But I am determined to make it over to the tallest, highest shelf, and pull down what is hidden from the shadow, intent on reading what is contained within.

The cover is dusty, and I stumble backward, the book's weight surprising despite its size. I am certain that what I am holding will tell me everything I need to know.

Just a volume from an ordinary encyclopedia, nothing really unusual at all, yet I lay it carefully on my bed as if it were scripture sent from above. The pages have the fragrance of something forgotten and untouched for years. Musty, damp, yet not totally unappealing. In fact, the scent of something soothing, almost recognizable.

The binding is blue, the cover letters gold, and the pages yellowed, almost transparent, surprisingly delicate, as if they might disintegrate at my touch. It is clear that no one has opened this particular book for a very long time.

I know it was once my father's, as are most of the volumes that I own; his name is inscribed on the opening page in shaky script. How many times have I studied these letters written in other books of his, traced what is engraved with my finger? I look down for a moment and then, after a minute or two, I slowly walk around the room, in the manner of a hunter approaching his prey. I am both nervous and exhilarated; there is nothing I cannot learn. Yet, is knowledge always useful? Can it also be disturbing, even terrifying?

I find the required page and rip it out. I will take notes and add them to the canvas scrapbook, which remains thin and incomplete. Only half a book recording half a life, half full.

B for bullet.
B for bereft.

I write carefully, slowly, checking to see that my facts are correct.

THIS IS WHAT A BULLET CAN DO
1. It can travel up to 2,800 feet per second.
2. It penetrates deeply, often causing shock and terrible damage.

3. It makes a much smaller hole when it enters the body than when it exits.
4. Sometimes a body's nervous system responds to the wound by overwhelming the brain's ability to cope, causing unconsciousness.
5. Comprehensive supportive treatment is necessary for survival and future health.
6. No matter how accurate the line of sight, wind or human error is possible. No matter how vulnerable the target, it still can be left intact.
7. The bullet's flight to its target is usually constant, its impact inescapable.

source: *Junior Encyclopedia of America*
reference: *Journal of the Internal Wound*

Why does it not surprise me to read that a bullet makes a much smaller hole when it enters the body than when it exits? That the initial impact is not as great as the eventual result?

I think of my scars from my own wounds. So tiny when the incisions were first made, but spreading larger and larger with every year of my growth. I think of my double and what scars he would have by now; I wonder exactly where he has gone.

I close the encyclopedia and sigh. The morning newspaper noted a particular gun had been used in the recent murders, a hunting or assault rifle with a scope that magnifies a target to increase accuracy. Apparently, according to the reporter, this kind of rifle is known to be used by militant survivalist groups, those who retreat or are rejected from their own communities, angry at the world at large. They live together in mountain hideouts and raise their children to be soldiers, training them how to attack aggressively, and to never retreat. There was one group in particular, noted in the newspaper last year, that interested me so greatly that I couldn't get it out of my mind.

It was a family of militants who lived in a cabin deep in the woods. Their home was stocked with rifles and the children were taught how to shoot. When the parents were arrested, the children stood their ground. They took up positions at the windows, guns drawn, apparently with no intention of surrendering, and they knew exactly how to protect each other's lives.

I try to remember what happened to them, whether the police succeeded in invading the house, or the children persevered by themselves.

When is it time for me to surrender, to give up all memory and turn away from my loss? Should I forget about my brother and the sacrifice asked of him at birth? Or is it possible that another is out there, a specter of myself? While I am not prone to believing in the occult, it is hard to ignore the signs. Mademoiselle once said that she saw the ghost of my father when she was dyeing her hair black one rainy afternoon.

"I had just squeezed the bottle on my roots, my dear, sitting right here at my vanity with a pink bib around my neck in case anything should drip on my dressing gown. You know, the lovely satin one you so admire."

She spun around to smile brightly at me, both hands slick with body oil, and then carefully dipped her elbows in a large jar of Vaseline, one by one. Next she pulled on her cotton gloves, carefully tugging at their hems, reminding me of a surgeon preparing for the first cut.

"Some may think that it is peculiar, darling, so you might not want to say a word, but he appeared right in front of me all of a sudden, here in this very room. The poor boy was wearing a silk ascot and smoking a pipe—I can even remember the scent, somewhat fruity and sweet. When I called out his name, he vanished into thin air, leaving nothing but a memory, something no one else would believe. And it is so odd that the clothes he wore were beautifully styled. When your father was alive, my dear, he refused to listen to me, dressing himself in old rags."

"Old rags?" I asked, surprised at the term.

She stood up slowly and pulled her bathrobe belt tight, then stroked her throat with a gloved index finger as if trying to locate a sudden pain. She was not wearing lipstick, so her mouth was ghostly white, and I noticed how she hunched forward, looking unusually small. My grandmother was a tiny woman, both in weight and in height, but at that moment she seemed to shrink even smaller right before my very eyes.

"Shush, child," she wheezed so softly that I barely could hear, "I don't want to discuss this any longer. I would like absolute silence for now."

Suddenly I remember mention of a silencer being used at the neighborhood crimes. No shots had been heard at any of the locations. The neighbors, shop owners, were interviewed, but no one reported anything, no noise of any kind.

Once again I open the encyclopedia and look up "gun silencers," but see only a reference to "gun suppressors." I turn the page and find myself wishing Mademoiselle had let me buy a computer like everybody else at my school. But she had fears about radiation and "mad scientists," insisting that computers and microwaves could do tremendous damage to the human immune system—that in years to come they would destroy one's body, making it permanently vulnerable to infection, unable to protect itself at all.

"One day you'll understand," she told me the very afternoon I had brought up the subject of technology all over again.

We were examining her duvet cover with an enormous gold-leaf magnifying glass, in search of invisible mites, Mademoiselle stretching forward from her damask pillow and I at the other end of the bed. Unfortunately I had just learned in science class that day that tiny bugs and mites were everywhere, even in our linens, and I had made the mistake of relaying this information to my grandmother, causing her alarm.

"The idea of mites is extremely distressing—it makes me ill to think about it—but don't fool yourself, my dear: modern science is even more dangerous than anything you might imagine or see with your own eyes. And radiation is the most lethal of all."

She sighed almost contentedly and leaned back carefully in her large bed.

A cool compress lay on her forehead, often used for her frequent headaches, and she suddenly looked exhausted, ancient, her face both frozen and animated at the same time, like that of a china doll, its worn features delicately composed but still somehow crude.

It was the end of the day and her makeup was melting, slowly sliding down her face in uneven streaks. I watched as it congealed beneath her chin.

"Don't let them talk you into anything, my dear. Don't trust the general public, don't let them do you harm." She was whispering softly and I could tell she would soon fall asleep. "Pour me another sip of sherry, and hand me my eye mask, will you, darling. I think it's time to switch off the lights."

I turn back to the encyclopedia's section on guns and continue taking notes. This is what I write:

SECRETS OF SILENCING
(HOW TO MAKE A SILENCER)
ENTER THE QUIET WORLD OF SILENCERS.

DISSIPATE EXPLOSION AT ITS SOURCE.
YOU CAN USE HOUSEHOLD ITEMS:
screen wire
soft drink containers
bottle caps
steel wool
PVC pipe
You can also put a potato at
the end of the barrel.

*There are many ways to completely muffle
all sound, but the echo always can be
heard by the shooter.
Silencers are the most devastating of devices.*

And so, at this moment, I suddenly know. It comes to me all at once; it becomes perfectly clear.

I will take my cue from the quiet world of silencers, and be devastatingly subdued. I will muffle all sound and not speak of my worst fears.

I will dissipate the possible explosion of what I might know.

I will be silent.

I will suppress all words.

I will not tell anybody anything, no matter what.

My challenge will be to protect my brother's shadow.

Now it is my turn to sacrifice.

In fact, until all of this is settled, someone apprehended and sent to jail, I will not say a word.

I will not respond when spoken to. I will not reveal anything I know.

I will refuse to cooperate.

I, too, will be adamant.

The boy seems more approachable today, and even apologizes for his strange behavior the morning before. Grace is relieved and promises herself to be careful about questioning Noah or pressing him to talk. The success of this first placement could mean future assignments, and it terrifies her to think of failing, of not being able to help those in need, to comfort and to heal. After all, she had saved all of her high school babysitting and waitressing money in order to take the necessary courses so that she could hold such a position. She had proudly hung the certificate in the middle of her bedroom wall.

But is she really being a help to this family or somehow making things worse? Should she stick to the structure of traditional care as outlined by all of her instructors, keeping a certain distance from family members? *Establish clear boundaries*, she had been told time and time again by her teachers. *Never risk becoming too involved with clients or relatives. Maintain balance. Remain compassionate but objective at the same time.* It really isn't her job to please Noah or keep him entertained, but to make sure he's safe and well taken care of during this difficult time. But remaining distant and formal were never her strong points; it seems unnatural to always be so removed, and Noah's apology this morning, no matter how tentative, heartens her. Grace hopes to see more signs of his progress in days to come and is all the more determined to concentrate on the job before her.

Still, he's so awfully thin, and seems so fearful, and she feels her heart careening each time he walks into a room. Always dressed neatly, usually in the same stiff khaki pants and meticulously ironed shirt, but always his head lowered, never looking all the way up into her face.

His leanness borders on the extreme, reminding her of photographs of starving children overseas, and although his sleeves are usually rolled all the way down, when he reaches out she can see the thinnest of wrists. Tiny, like a baby's, delicate, like someone sick. His skin colorless, his body limp, when he moves there's barely any sound. He walks hunched over, taking small, hobbled steps like an old man, but has the voice of a child, soft like a little girl's. And she wonders at the choice of haircut, his head shaved so closely that the skull is scattered with small nicks of dried blood, the back of his neck hollowing out like a narrow crater when he bends down.

She would like to reach out to touch him, but knows that he will withdraw, even leave the room. She must watch her step carefully so as not to spook him. She knows this, yet it's still hard.

And then there's the matter of the grandmother, the old woman who's taken care of him for so long. He barely talks of her; in fact, she realizes suddenly, he hasn't mentioned her name since the very first evening. None of Grace's instructors or classes have prepared her for this kind of situation and Grace doesn't know the correct thing to do. But she does understand that children need structure and become upset when their world suddenly changes, when they feel abandoned and out of control. Perhaps when this is all over and Noah finds familiar stability once again, perhaps he'll manage better and begin to flourish. For now, she worries about him and isn't quite sure how to help.

She notices that the boy lingers by his grandmother's door as if the old woman might actually call out to him. And then notices how his shoulders slump, how he shuffles slowly away.

And when a few neighbors stop by to express their concern, Noah hides upstairs. When the phone rings, he refuses to answer it or talk with anyone at all.

But today Grace is a bit encouraged. At least there's some conversation between the two of them, even if it's over this grisly murder. She still feels mixed about discussing the crime with him; but then again, he is thirteen, after all, and seems determined to find out about it anyway. Kids these days are a lot smarter than you imagine, she thinks, and much more knowledgeable of the world.

In any case, the incident seems a means for them to communicate, and in all honesty, the lurid news fascinates, obsesses, terrifies her. That such random violence can happen is mysterious in the first place, but to have the murder take place so close to this house, in the same neighborhood—well, it is both compelling and repulsive. She finds herself drawn to the facts and disgusted at the same time. And it seems similar with the boy, who rushes to gather new information, but then seems literally sickened once he learns anything of significance at all.

Of course, Grace is familiar with violence, with the suddenness of it, the impact of crime. Curious, considering her own heartbreak, that the murders interest her so, curious that we are so often fascinated with the unthinkable.

She feels herself suddenly stiffen with memory of that afternoon two years ago when her mother rushed through the front door, dropping her coat on the floor and wrapping her arms around her, how Grace pushed her away, how she wouldn't talk to anyone, how she wouldn't speak for weeks, wouldn't move from her bed.

They hadn't let her see him in intensive care later. She hadn't even been able to say good-bye.

Her mother grew silent and withdrawn after he was gone, sleeping late into the day and then working into the early hours of morning. Mother and daughter barely saw each other then, their only communication hastily scribbled notes left on the kitchen counter.

Grace,
We need skim milk and American cheese. See you later.
—Mom

The disposal is broken. Should I call the super?
—Grace

Grace,
His number is on the refrigerator magnet. Have a good day.
—Mom

The super was here at noon but has to come back tomorrow with a wrench. Will be home by 10:00.

— Grace

Grace didn't know why she bothered to let her mother know where she was going or when she would be back. She was always in bed hours before her mother made it home and would squeeze her eyes shut as the key turned in the front door latch, praying for morning when the daylight would wipe away dark images. At dawn she would rise, throw her old plaid wool bathrobe over her shoulders, and head downstairs for breakfast.

Only food consoled her.

She was suddenly ravenous all the time, eager to tear into platefuls, compelled to rip open boxes of cookies, crackers, to scoop up mounds of ice cream, pudding, and cake. Fried chicken at midnight. Frozen cheesecake at 1:00 A.M. Raspberry jam and graham crackers at dawn and a can of vanilla icing by the time she showered for work.

She'd barely speak to anyone. Sometimes old friends would call, even an old boyfriend or two, but she would decline, soon refusing to answer the phone. She didn't have any interest in the hottest movie stars, the newest music, the latest styles. For weeks, then months, she wasn't interested in anything at all.

Sleep was a thing of the past. Had she ever slept peacefully? Her life before loss seemed distant, a dream, something she had only wished for and once imagined. Had there ever been a little boy? Had he ever giggled, looking up at her, had he ever called out her name?

Soon the grief and yearning became an odd kind of tonic, comforting and familiar. Weekends, she would stay in her nightgown until the afternoon. Breakfast would be heated up—Chinese takeout from the day before, washed down with a pint of chocolate milk, and the cycle would begin all over again. Sundays, her mother would stumble into the kitchen at noon, raw-eyed and exhausted with sorrow herself. She would just stare at her daughter and sigh.

Grace's need was bottomless. Strange, most

would not have an appetite under those circumstances. Not Grace—she found herself furiously consuming anything she could find, anything at all.

No. She will not think of this, better to put it out of her mind.

It's time to make lunch for the boy, anyway. What will Noah have today, for heaven's sake, with all of his strict rules about every ingredient of each and every meal? She looks in the refrigerator. It's still practically empty, despite her daily efforts to fill it with more fresh groceries. A package of chicken breasts is defrosting and she prods it with a finger to see if it's soft. Maybe some soup with vegetables. Strange that the boy won't eat refined products, but seems to accept meat, if it is a lean cut or skinless poultry. Odd, you would think that with all his notions, he'd be vegetarian or even vegan.

Her own little brother wouldn't touch red meat, with the exception of hamburgers, and she would make him endless peanut butter sandwiches to make sure he got the necessary protein.

He insisted that the sandwiches be crustless

and cut into small squares. A lot of good all those sandwiches did him.

Enough.

Grace can't remember all of this right now—she has one more day not to think about it. One more day before she has to make the call.

Suddenly she feels exhausted and leans against the refrigerator door. A page from the newspaper drifts from the kitchen table onto the floor at her feet, and as she bends to pick it up, she feels a sharp pang. The headlines of the murder float before her once again, with an old, grainy photograph of the slain doctor on his front porch, smiling and waving. Grace wonders about his family, what they're feeling, and then wonders what she is feeling herself.

Does she want her own brother's murderer caught?

Yes.

Does she want justice?

Absolutely.

Does she want revenge?

No.

Is she angry?

Maybe.

Mostly what Grace feels is numbness, a frozen gate that slides down inside and then snaps into place. Actually she finds herself feeling little, conscious that something keeps her separated from fury. The world continues to roll on slowly by, but without specifics. The colors of flowers, the scent of coffee, flavors, noises, and shapes—none of it is available to her anymore.

Although food continues to comfort her, it's the texture of it, the fullness of her stomach after finishing, that makes her feel better, and not the taste. All of this gone from her life as if she's come out of a serious illness with her senses left impaired, unable to experience much of anything anymore. This is why this job is so important, and why she chose this career. For some reason she thinks that helping others, especially other children, will help nudge her back to life; maybe it's a way to stop thinking about herself and the pitiful size of her baby brother's grave.

No matter. She's here, isn't she? She's following the cliché "Take it day by day." There are others here who need her and she'll try to offer them comfort in every possible way.

Tomorrow morning, before thinking about the telephone call, Grace will bake the boy fresh blueberry muffins and hunt for whole wheat flour and brown sugar at the corner store, avoiding the shelves filled with cookies, chips, and candy. She'll follow Noah's lead and only buy the healthiest of ingredients; she'll cook for him as a mother would, focusing on his nutrition while preparing concoctions impossible to resist.

While he's still sleeping, Grace will stand by the warm oven, stirring slowly, her muscles sore from beating the thick batter with a wooden spoon. She'll pour the mixture into small paper cups and then place them in a silver muffin tin, also just bought brand-new.

The boy will awaken slowly, the fragrance of her recipe floating upstairs like a magical potion. He'll pull his bathrobe over his thin shoulders and sleepily follow the aroma. He'll come downstairs to the kitchen, where she will be silent, waiting and hoping for words.

Liam's case was closed two years ago today.

Grace picks up the beige receiver from the princess telephone in the upstairs hallway and pulls the cord through her bedroom door. She wishes desperately to be at home in her own apartment where she has some real privacy. There's just no room here, no space for her at all; each day of her stay, the house seems to shrink, her already substantial frame to grow. She feels as if she's an adolescent cramming herself into the coat closet, making secret calls to her friends when she should be doing homework or chores. After all, that really wasn't so many years ago, although it seems like forever.

But she doesn't want Noah to overhear. It's the last thing he needs to know.

The dial tone is overwhelmingly loud, and Grace realizes the volume is set high, as if for someone hard of hearing. Of course, the old woman must have had trouble and adjusted the sound just so. The receiver smells like a combination of disinfectant and something else— liquor and perfume? She turns the volume down by digging her fingernail into the small ridged button; she takes a deep breath and waits.

"Petersburgh Police. Is this an emergency?" The voice on the other end sounds like a child, barely audible.

"No, no," she quickly replies, "not an emergency. But I was wondering if I might talk with Detective Stallman. This is Grace Rush. He'll know who I am."

"Detective Stallman?"

"Yes." She is getting impatient and feels her face flush red.

"Hold, please."

Her heart is pounding.

"Petersburgh Police. Is this an emergency?" It is the same girlish voice on the other end.

"No, I just told you. This is not an emergency.

I am calling for Detective Stallman. Is he in? This is Grace Rush."

There is a pause.

Please don't put me on hold, she prays.

"Detective Stallman? I'm sorry, he's no longer with us. The detective retired from the department last month."

She feels faint and starts to sit on the bed, then realizes the phone cord won't stretch quite that far. "But it's important that I speak to him. Someone must have his number, some way to contact him."

"Please hold."

Grace squeezes her chest with one hand. She tries to inhale slowly, and then exhale again, but her breathing is uncontrollable and her head spins. What if she has a heart attack right here in this room? She'll die, never knowing the answer. And the boy, Noah, what would become of him? He'd find her huge body on his guest room floor.

"Mrs. Rush?" The voice returns.

"Miss Rush." Grace exhales slowly.

"Sorry, ma'am. Now, how may I help you?"

"I'm calling for Detective Stallman. You said

he's retired, but that's not possible. It's important that I speak with him. Please don't put me back on hold."

"Detective Stallman is no longer with us, ma'am."

"But do you have a number for him? Someplace I can call?"

"We are not at liberty to release such information."

Grace hears a shrill ringing in her ears. She finds it difficult to speak.

"Please," she eventually pleads. The blank walls around her are reeling. "Someone's got to help me. They never said he was about to retire. No one contacted me. How can this have happened? He's the only one I know to talk with."

"Would you like me to connect you to his replacement, Detective Hinkle? I do believe he is in."

"Please." She sits on the floor awkwardly, trying to put her head between her knees to avoid feeling faint, but her stomach protrudes, its cumbersome mass in the way.

They promised to contact her with any

information, they promised to keep her updated, they promised that Detective Stallman would call.

Liam's is a cold case.

She knows that.

How she hates those words.

"Detective Hinkle here. How may I help you?"

She opens and closes her mouth, but cannot speak.

"Hello, Detective Hinkle. Is anyone there?"

"Please," she finally says weakly. "Please, can you help me? My brother was murdered and I don't know what to do."

He will call her back. He promises. He is not familiar with the case. Detective Stallman did not leave any information. He has not even read the file.

He is sorry. He understands.

Sometimes cases can be reopened, but it's unusual. Exceptions are made, but they are rare. He will do everything possible. Not to worry. Be patient. It is such a shame, such a sorrow.

Grace slams the phone down on the floor and

then kicks it across the room. She rocks from side to side and then rests her head against the wall.

She wakes up from her nap two hours later, her head filled with confusing images from a most peculiar dream, her mouth soaked in bitterness and her body shaking with the cold. Why, for heaven's sake, why is this godforsaken house always freezing and why can't she find the thermostat to adjust the air? Noah's no help, just shaking his head and looking down, and she finds it strange that he doesn't know how to keep his own house warm.

Grace shudders and pulls the blanket up around her shoulders. What exactly had she dreamed about and why so disturbing, knotted bits of color still drifting through her mind like tangled thread? She closes her eyes and then opens them again. Yes, now she remembers. She had been dreaming of the tarot, the familiar symbols swirling before her like colorful ghosts. The Hermit, the Magician, the Empress. . . . Death.

Clearly, the news of the sniper and his tarot card is on her mind. How odd that this murderer has chosen to use such an ancient practice as a means of communicating his own madness. How odd that she's even thinking about this at all. She blinks and tries to will away all remnants of her dream. After all, it's already 8:00 P.M.; she has responsibilities to complete and there is still dinner to be made. Suddenly Grace is alarmed. She's overslept and neglected her duties. She sits up quickly, reaching for her sweater.

It's dark outside and the house is eerily quiet. She walks by Noah's bedroom door, carefully listening for signs of life.

"Noah," she calls quietly, her nose pressed against the wall. "Noah, are you awake? Have you eaten? Can I make you anything?"

She pushes the door carefully with one finger, surprised when it squeaks open a few inches. After several moments her eyes adjust to the dark and she blinks twice. The room is small and square, lined with shelves and shelves of books of every shape and size. When Grace had been in Noah's room the day before, she somehow hadn't noticed the sheer number of volumes filling each and every corner.

It's dark, difficult to see clearly, the blinds pulled all the way down, but she is able to make out a wide bed up against one wall.

There, the boy sleeps, whispering in his dreams, blankets tossed off to the side, his slight frame barely visible in voluminous white pajamas.

Grace longs to sit down beside him and cradle his scarred head, but she knows the importance of keeping her distance.

Noah sighs suddenly, weakly calling out in his sleep.

He is curled up tightly in the fetal position, his coiled shadow darkening the other side of the double bed.

· DAY FIVE ·

NOAH

It is day five, and still no one has been apprehended.

News of both shootings fills the paper's
metro section and there are even more details
about the murders in the following pages. Strange
how there can be so much published incidental
information, yet nothing about the sniper himself. It is as if he flickers, indistinct, on the fringes
of other lives, always present yet permanently
invisible, never to be identified or found.

I sit in the kitchen as Nurse Grace prepares
breakfast, the crackling heat from the oven burning my eyes, tiny incandescent spots of light suddenly appearing before me. I blink again and
they are gone, but their random, delicate pattern
has already been etched into my pupils. I realize,

with irritation, that for the next hour or so, and also maybe even later tonight, when I try to sleep, each time I close my eyes, these same glimmerings will flit throughout my vision, as if permanently logged into the memory of sight.

Once observed, an image becomes enduring, forever coloring one's vision, impossible to disregard. This is an unsettling fact, but one that is unfortunately, undisputedly true.

Even that which you wish to forget, that which you attempt to ignore, is always present. The discolored faces leering in the nighttime, the howling wind that throbs in your ear on a calm summer day, the manner in which a familiar face slowly turns away from you, someone you might know, even a beloved, the frigid silence you try so hard to fill.

The bullet's flight to its target is constant, its impact inescapable.

Suddenly I am aware of a smarting at the corner of both eyes, and feel two stinging teardrops carve a path down my cheeks. Probably the result of the intensely dry heat slithering through the oven door. I wipe my face quickly, somehow thinking of Mademoiselle, how she prided herself in never having learned to cook; in fact, I don't remember my grandmother ever once having used this stove.

"Raw food is the best," she would tell me again and again, almost the way a parent endlessly repeats the same fairy tale to an enchanted child. "It helps the body eliminate all excess, all but what is absolutely required. Make me a salad with endive for dinner tonight, will you, my darling, and please do not forget the grated carrots for added flavor and color."

How many salads did Mademoiselle and I eat together over the years, she nibbling delicately, soundlessly, from the paper plate on the bed tray laid out neatly in front of her, and I sitting by her side in the wooden straight-back chair, curling the cold endive with my tongue until it snapped back against the roof of my mouth? We would each sip slowly from tall, identical water glasses, mine usually filled with clear tonic, and Mademoiselle's with sherry or some other fragrant adult drink. Sometimes I would prepare two small bowls of baby lettuces, adding the tiniest of cherry tomatoes and slivered bean sprout, a plate of melba toast thinly spread with cottage cheese as a supplement to the cold meal. Every once in a while, my grandmother would prefer romaine for her salad, claiming that it was good for her digestion and for the luminance of her skin. Most nights, however, we would simply sift our plastic forks through a neat mound of iceberg lettuce chopped into tidbits and topped with a dusting of sharp, dark green chive.

Once a week, on Wednesdays, Mademoiselle and I examined the faded take-out menu from the gourmet delicatessen down the street, and ordered salmon poached in fish broth, or grilled chicken on a bed of blanched greens. The food would be delivered right to our doorstep, along with a large brown cardboard carton containing weekly supplies of bottled drink. Mademoiselle always requested that I carry that particular item upstairs and store it directly in the large hall linen closet, as the downstairs kitchen cupboards were unfortunately too shallow to accommodate such bulk.

I would rest the unwieldy box on my shoulder gingerly as I carried it up the narrow stairs, its weight daunting, the pressure almost unbearable against my splintering joints and bones. I would always be afraid something fragile inside might be broken, and listen anxiously to the bottles rub against their container, the glass clinking together in a mournful chime.

"Oh, my goodness, I don't think I will ever be able to eat again," my grandmother would chant after those particular Wednesday meals, patting the blankets surrounding her belly. "Please don't ever let me eat so much again, my dear, even if I beg and plead."

Why, I would sometimes wonder idly to myself, why such value placed on staying so tiny, so small, almost not even present at all? Why is the human flesh so rejected, almost considered evil, more deadly than illness, more despicable than sin? I would look down at my own hands, my wrists and arms, marveling at the maze of narrow veins poking up from beneath, my colorless skin sheer, almost watery, my ragged small bones revealed right through an invisible shell. I would feel uncomfortably fragile, breakable, vulnerable to annihilation then, a boy poised for evaporation, positioned to disappear, brittle skin and skeleton easily crumbled into dust.

But then I would have to reassure my desperate grandmother, emphasizing the slimness of her shape, and complimenting her girlish figure. She would smile back up at me, her delicate features almost twitching with delight, her lipstick faded after the consumption of her dinner, her thin lips hardly visible, difficult to discern among the loose pockets of wrinkled skin. I remember noticing the shininess of her forehead, slick with face grease and stuck with tufts of blue-black hair from the damp, wiry bangs crumpled above.

Would her narrow eyes roll back in her head for a moment before they closed, or was that my imagination?

I remember my grandmother's exact expression those nights, right before she lost consciousness and fell into her characteristically deep sleep. She would have a half smile engraved on her face, her features somehow lopsided, muddled, as if they had slipped in entirely opposite directions, like jumbled parts of a child's puzzle that needed to be slid back into place. I would shiver when I noticed that the slits in her eyes were still a fraction open, the lids fluttering like someone in grave danger, their erratic, fragile motion apparent even after she had most definitely drifted away.

I would gently lay my grandmother's satin night mask over her tiny face and shudder as I left the room, treading carefully, intent on not being heard, determined not to disturb any little last thing.

I sigh and take in the scene surrounding me now. How dramatically my life has changed this past week. Once it was a quiet house defined by order, routine; now all of a sudden it is noisy, chaotic, without any perceptible structure. Just look at Nurse Grace as she bustles mindlessly around the kitchen, whipping up some concoction made with apples and honey, insisting that the ingredients are all natural and wholesome. And poor Mademoiselle, as if she had never lived here at all, all of her rules forgotten, unable to object or even utter a single word.

Trying to ignore Nurse Grace's clatter, I examine the paper for more details of the crimes. On page three, a female psychic claims to have seen two vampires sucking blood from their prey, and on page four there is an interview with the owner of a store who sold a rifle to a "suspicious character" several days before, but no descriptive information is given. I scan the paper further. A pharmacist, an eyewitness to the previous shooting, is interviewed on page five; he claims to have seen a young girl fleeing from the scene of the last murder, but the police have apparently discounted his story, as his account differs substantially from those of others interviewed.

Out of the corner of my eye, I notice Nurse Grace licking a spoon, and I grimace. Is there no end to her slovenliness, her greedy, haphazard tasting of ingredients, the careless disposal of dishes in the sink, her collection of spices and traces of flour left on the counter like clues on a lost child's trail? The kitchen, usually quiet and spotless, brims with commotion, the sounds of

141

gruesome things being chopped into little bits and thrown into pots bubbling heartlessly on the stove.

At first, when Nurse Grace arrived, I followed her all about, trying to pick up the mess left in her wake, attempting to gather the remnants of forgotten peach pits, seeds from an orange, mysterious batter left to harden on the stove. I would throw out crumpled pieces of paper towel, empty boxes of strawberry Jell-O and crackers, cartons of juice and milk, curls of pasta, dots of tomato sauce, old tea bags drying out on the windowsill and leaving a stain permanently carved into the wood. I emptied the sink of dirty dishes, scoured the oven after her baking, even realigned the bottles of her newly purchased spices when they lay abandoned and sprawling in the small drawer.

In the beginning, I found this challenge daunting—shadowing Nurse Grace without being noticed, eliminating all evidence of her cooking, of her existence, without her even knowing I am there. But after a few days I soon get tired of the whole process, preferring to ignore the entire mess and distract myself with things of greater importance.

Still, watching her now gleefully dot the skinned and quartered apples with sharp cloves, then smother them with such a heavy blanket of thick honey that the sides of the pan drip ruthlessly onto the spotless Formica table, it is hard not to stand up and call for mercy. It is hard not to scream at the top of my lungs and whip out the mop bucket in defense, along with my extrawide nylon broom. And why Nurse Grace must prepare this evening's dinner so early in the day is beyond me—she says she wants it completed so that it will be ready whenever we are hungry later, but her eagerness seems somehow ill-mannered, inappropriate, as if she has never learned to wait.

And yet here is the newspaper before me, certainly of greater concern, crammed with reports of the shootings, full of interviews with the police, with criminal profilers, acquaintances of the deceased, even shop owners near where the murders took place. My eye catches a photograph at the bottom of one page, a balding man in a white shirt in front of a cluster of microphones. Another doctor updating the public about the condition of the most recent victim. The article is entitled "Talking Trauma: A Layman's Guide to the Grisly Details."

"Noah," Nurse Grace calls, her mouth clearly full of some morsel obstructing her speech, "please help me with this."

It is evident that she finds the tasting of her dishes a necessary step in the entire brutal process of elaborate meal preparations. I can almost hear the voracious smacking of lips, of her gnawing on an innocent morsel not quite yet cooked, intercepted by her gluttonous mouth, incapable of escape.

I sigh and pretend not to listen. I am not eager to get up or to move the newspaper from my lap.

"This tray of baked apples. It's burning hot."

I turn to find Nurse Grace bending into the oven, her broad rump quivering, sturdy legs shaking with anticipation. She is wearing a blue denim skirt with an apron around her huge waist, and its tie loosens, dropping off to one hip. Her hem lifts over the back of her knees and I see a twist of puffy blue veins choking two trunks of loose flesh.

I look away quickly.

Something drips from the pan, spattering with a sizzle on the floor.

"Noah?" Her voice is insistent, more of a statement than a question.

How did I end up in this situation?

How can it be that I am victim to such disorder and disarray?

I have no choice but to stand up and help her. I have no choice but to set the newspaper down. And as I walk over to her side, large oven mitts flapping over my small hands, I am reminded of a fairy tale and a witch bent over another oven, two lost children tempted by sweets and trails of crumbs.

Nurse Grace is bending into the hot stove and I make sure to keep my distance from her warmth, offering my help but not stepping close enough to be grabbed.

The clock on the oven notes the time as 9:00 A.M., and I am suddenly amused. We have both been awake for one solid hour and Nurse Grace has not yet noticed that I refuse to utter a sound.

She takes the mitts from my hands without shifting position and the heat from the oven suddenly flares up, making me stagger backward into a waiting kitchen chair.

My eyes are burning all over again, and for a minute I think my vision will be permanently impaired, but then the room comes back into focus, and I remember the morning's news once more.

The Petersburgh Gazette is still spread out on the table before me, and I reach for the front page. The article is particularly troubling, as a young child has been the last victim to be attacked.

TALKING TRAUMA: A LAYMAN'S GUIDE TO THE GRISLY DETAILS

Last week, a 14-year-old student in Geneva County became the sixth known target of a sniper's bullet.

Victor Frank, M.D., chief trauma surgeon at Petersburgh Children's Hospital, discussed the child's wound and prognosis at a news conference. The doctor outlined the consequences of sudden injury as follows:

Head and Spine
Comatose or paralyzed patients face the longest odds. When collections of blood from impact or so-called "foreign bodies" are surgically removed, the danger isn't over. Brain swelling often develops over several days. The higher the velocity of the original impact, the more likely cerebral edema is to develop. And while there are ways to limit the effects of brain swelling, there are no proven cures.

I look up from the paper for a moment as if memorizing what I have read. *Comatose or paralyzed patients face the longest odds.*

I picture the stricken child immobile, frozen in his hospital bed. Does he try to talk, or is he in a full-blown coma? Does he attempt to move his limbs, or is his injury permanent, life-threatening—will he ever be able to fully function again?

I turn back to the article.

Chest

At the top of what trauma surgeons call the "cone of death" is the head and neck; the base is the heart and the "great blood vessels"—the aorta and vena cava, which run vertically through the center of the chest. Penetrating injuries here are literally a race against time. Only those who get help quickly can have their blood restored and lacerations of heart or blood vessels repaired. Since the heart may become severely contused or bruised, the mainstay of treatment is largely supportive. But, as with the young victim of last week's shooting, once surgery is finished, survival is out of the doctors' hands. The healthier the patient, and the more supportive the care, the greater the odds that the patient will weather internal damage.

Shock and Infection

The true medical state of shock exists when there is insufficient blood to meet the needs of the body. The body responds by trying to clamp down on blood flow to the brain, heart, lungs, liver, and kidneys. Unless these blood components can be transfused fairly quickly, the cascade of bleeding can itself prove to be fatal. As a secondary effect, in the first days and weeks out, this also depletes the body's ability to fight infection. Someone who makes it through initial surgery, therefore, also faces the prospect of an overwhelming infection.

The prospect of a child, someone my own age, suffering such internal damage and overwhelming infection is deeply disturbing to me. How does one ever resume the courage to live after such trauma, such significant internal injury, and is it possible that a complete recovery can ever be made, or will his future be permanently impaired, the days ahead to be half imagined, half lived?

Will the child lie there forever listless, in a suspended state of body and mind, alive yet not really living, his heart pumping weakly, while the rest of him slowly withers away inside?

I put the paper down and sigh.

I notice the kitchen table is set for our meal. Soon it will be expected that I will be hungry, and that I will finish everything on my plate.

Nurse Grace is chattering so over breakfast, it is not difficult to remain silent.

"I'm so pleased you like the apples," she fairly chortles, reaching to spoon some more steaming sauce over my serving. "I always loved them myself as a child."

Shaking my head is all that is needed for her to stop her ladling, but she withdraws her arm tentatively, as if I might suddenly change my mind.

"I tried to think of something that would tempt you, Noah, something nourishing and hot. I realize that you avoid certain ingredients, and I'm really trying to respect this. At the same time, it's important that you stay fortified with foods full of vitamins and proteins necessary for the health of a growing boy, for someone your age."

She stops talking for a moment in order to

spear a hunk of dripping apple with her own fork. I must admit, the breakfast is oddly tasty, the sharpness of the apple and the coating of honey a surprisingly agreeable combination. And the temperature of the dish is also pleasing, the soft fruit and warm syrup soothing, almost medicinal. I eat slowly, little bites at first, but then find myself not objecting when Nurse Grace slides another glistening orb onto my plate.

"You know," she continues, chewing loudly, "I have another recipe that I just read in a magazine, something you really might like. It just occurs to me that, since the apples are such a success, I should try baking some of my pies. Don't worry," she continues as I raise an eyebrow, "I'll make sure to use brown sugar and whole wheat flour. Still, there are many options: blueberry, peach, cherry, even rhubarb. Of course, I'll stay away from those filled with cream. What kinds of fruit do you like?"

I shrug and she smiles.

"Good. Well, I'll just find out what's freshest at the market and we'll go from there. Maybe you'd even like to help me, learn how to bake a real old-fashioned pie. How about it, Noah? One day you will be cooking all on your own, or for your very own family, and it's important for you to learn some of the basics. Come on, what do you think? I'll go shopping tomorrow, and we can bake in the afternoon."

Needless to say, the idea is not exactly appealing to me, but since there is no way to forcefully object, I just shrug again, and taste a dollop of cloved honey sticking to the corner of my lip.

Surprising how no one really cares when you refuse to utter a single word.

It is not until 4 P.M. that Nurse Grace notices something is awry. I spend the afternoon upstairs, reading the collected works of Ursula K. Le Guin and avoiding the dreaded luncheon ordeal by feigning sleep.

Around noon I hear my door open and Nurse Grace's heavy breathing, but then, thank goodness, the door is pulled shut again. I open my eyes and sigh with relief. Almost an entire day to myself, alone in my room. I pull several new books from the shelf and pile them up on my bed.

But when she knocks loudly again later in the afternoon and then calls out my name, I still don't answer, so she opens the door just a crack once more, and actually looks quite alarmed.

"Noah, are you all right? Aren't you feeling well?"

I am lying on my back, holding Mary Shelley's *Frankenstein* above me in midair, my favorite position for reading. Somehow, keeping the book at a distance helps me focus, and when I stretch my arms out over my face, the text gripped tightly with both hands, the words on the page seem clearer. The print darkens, enlarges, almost becoming three dimensional, as if printed only for my own particular two eyes. I own the hardback version of this specific book, and my arms are sore from its weight, tired from being extended so far.

"Noah?"

My whole body bristles.

To tell the truth, at that moment I don't know quite what to do. How am I to communicate to her that I no longer have words, that my sincere intention is not to speak once more, if ever again? Needless to say, I do nothing, I do not turn to her, or move a single inch.

Nurse Grace is silent for a moment, then suddenly rushes over to my bed, sits down right beside me, and presses a moist hand to my forehead. I try to roll over quickly, barely escaping her clammy, unfamiliar touch.

"Noah," she asks again, "are you okay? Are you sick? Is something bothering you? Should I call the doctor?"

It is clear that the woman is not about to give up or to leave me alone.

"Noah?"

With some misgivings, but it does seem a necessary compromise of a sort, just this one time, I reach over to my bedstand for a piece of paper and a pencil. This is to be the very last time that I will write an explanation of my choice. Luckily there is a small yellow pad and a blue felt-tip pen in the top drawer, given to me some years ago as a Christmas present from Mademoiselle. My grandmother always encouraged me to keep comprehensive and copious lists of household necessities to be bought at the store and chores to be completed by the end of the day. The top page of the pad includes three items.

1. Change bath towels.
2. Dust television.
3. Shake out door mat, then sweep under it and look for dead leaves.

Mademoiselle hired a cleaning lady to come in once a week, but she preferred that I stay on top of the day-to-day activities required to keep a house clean and free of mindless disarray. I remember why I had written these three chores down on that particular morning: I had not completed my assignments the morning before, and Mademoiselle had not been pleased.

I rip of the top page off the pad and fold it neatly in half. It is clear that I do not need this list right now or ever again.

I feel Nurse Grace's eyes upon me, and yet I make sure to take my time. This is what I write.

I am fine. This is to be the last time that I will write.

After all, there is no reason to upset the woman. That is hardly my point at all. In fact, my silence has nothing to do with her. For now I have more weighty matters on my mind.

Nurse Grace glances at the note for a moment, then gives me a confused, startled look.

"I'm glad that you are fine, Noah, but is there some reason you are writing instead of communicating with speech?"

I shrug and look down.

"Is it your throat? Do you have a sore throat? Are you coming down with a cold?" She tries, once again, to feel my forehead but I squirm quickly away. "Noah"—her voice is raspy, a mixture of anxiety and irritation— "please say something to me, anything at all. Has something in particular recently upset you? Or are you playing some silly game? You're really beginning to scare me."

It seems to me that a health care professional might be a bit more composed, and not fall apart at the slightest provocation, over the insignificant silence of an inconsequential boy.

Silencers are the most devastating of devices.

I take the paper from her and smooth it carefully with one hand. Perhaps one more note would be necessary and would not constitute giving in. This time, in my clearest printing, I write:

I am fine. Please just leave me alone.
This really is the last time I will write.

She studies my note for what seems like a long time, then takes the pen from my hand.

I AM FINE TOO,
she writes in bold print,
BUT I WILL NOT LEAVE YOU ALONE.

Terrific, I think to myself. One would imagine that silence would be enough of a signal, enough of a clue. One would think someone would get the message and not persist. But clearly Nurse Grace will be a challenge, a woman not to be quickly dismissed.

This will not be as easy as I had assumed.

I stare down at her handwriting, shamelessly large and bold, then crumple the paper tightly in my hand until it is nothing but a small ball.

"Dinner's at six," she announces quietly, rubbing a large circular stain on her skirt. "Orange chicken with apricots and currants. I think you'll find it pretty tasty."

The floor trembles as she shuffles out of the room, the plush carpet not thick enough to stifle the impact of her exit, of her impressive weight.

· DAY SIX ·

NOAH

Another shooting, another headline.

This time the victim is a woman, a mother, middle-aged with three small children. A teacher, much beloved—there are written testimonies to that. Grace shakes her head and hands the newspaper right to me; she says nothing, but her face is solemn and it is clear that she is upset.

Dinner the evening before was not exactly pleasant either, the silence between us uncomfortable and her irritation with me noticeable. But we managed to get through it, slowly chewing together, the crunchy glaze from the chicken melting on our tongues, until eventually Nurse Grace chose to ignore my refusal to communicate, sighing heavily and speaking right out loud. It is a similar experience this morning: after a few minutes of quiet, the woman just cannot help but to say something, to begin a conversation in which I will not be engaged, at least not literally, with breath and with words.

"It's unbelievable that they still can't catch this lunatic," she says, shaking her head, inhaling sharply, and stirring my oatmeal with one hand. "What with all of the police out there, all the manpower, even the FBI. Not exactly reassuring, is it, when you rely on these officials for your safety and well-being. Not very reassuring at all. We should be able to take our personal safety for granted—we shouldn't have to be scared of opening the front door."

I notice that Nurse Grace is adorning the cereal with something unfamiliar, absentmindedly scattering small pieces with her fingers as if feeding park pigeons or a nest of baby birds. I peer over the bowl to determine exactly what has been dropped inside.

"Just leftover dried apricots I saved from last night's dinner. Don't worry, Noah, I'm not going to poison you with refined sugar or anything like that."

Her sarcasm is evident. Certainly, Nurse Grace is not pleased with me this morning. It is not hard to see that she is impatient with my resolution to proceed without words. I try not to be bothered, picking up the paper and scanning it for new information.

This recent shooting took place in a parking lot, in broad daylight, in front of a department store just a few miles from here. I shudder. Once again there is an eyewitness, someone who thought he saw a young boy fleeing the scene of the crime on foot, the vague description given similar to the others before: someone slim, no taller than five foot four inches, weighing just over one hundred pounds. No mention of hair color or clothing. No mention of distinguishing features or any real evidence left behind. Not even another tarot card to be found.

Still, the accounts are consistent. There is simply no two ways about it: the descriptions fit me to a tee.

Probably just a silly coincidence, probably happenstance of the most superficial sort, and yet, I cannot help but secretly wonder—part of me cannot help but be afraid.

Is someone just like me out there, someone roaring a murderous revenge?

And what if his anger includes the lone survivor, the twin chosen to live, the one left to take his unfortunate place?

Long ago, there was a procedure, a permanent fissure that included lacerations of the heart. There was a cascade of bleeding that proved to be fatal, a sudden shock when his body's needs no longer could be met.

Sacrifice surgery. What cold, unforgiving words.

My stomach tightens. The oatmeal curdles suddenly, midway down.

It begins to rain outside, at first just a little, but then I hear a clap of thunder, the back door banging as if being shoved open and then shut again, and a sudden whining of sirens racing down the street out front. All lights in the house dim for a moment, a sudden shadow flickers—maybe just Nurse Grace's distorted profile outlined on the opposite kitchen wall.

But when I turn to look for her, she is standing by the oven, all the way on the other side of the room, stirring something in a kettle with her long curved spoon. She brushes back a loose strand of hair from her forehead, and then another sticking to an enormous, swollen cheek, and looks over to me, flashing a ghastly smile. Do I hear her mumbling something under her breath, something garbled, not easily understood, or is it someone else's small voice calling out pitifully for my help?

The doors on the uppermost kitchen cupboards rattle as if something is trying to emerge from within.

A crack of lightening, more thunder, and then the whole house trembles.

I hold on to the edge of the table with both hands and squeeze my eyes shut. It is only a brief, faceless summer storm, flexing its invisible muscles, incapable of ripping an entire dwelling off the ground. It is impossible for this torrent to blow its way through the protection of a thoroughly walled house and swallow a quaking half boy.

I know all of this, and yet . . .

It feels as if the downpour is permanent, the deluge endless, that this outburst will never end, life as we know it obliterated. Two by two they went, two by two they survived.

The water heating up on the stove begins to bubble, and Nurse Grace slowly pours a steaming cup of bitter coffee into her enormous black enameled mug.

The woman is clever, I will definitely give her that.

When the storm finally weakens and breakfast is finished, and all of Nurse Grace's dishes are licked clean, she ushers me into the living room before I have the opportunity to escape.

It is clear she is someone not to be underestimated, not to be taken for granted in any sense at all. Nurse Grace is a surprise to me, not simply a simpering healthcare provider with the typical bleeding heart, not only someone eager to offer healing without an agenda of her own. No, this is an unusual woman, maybe even a worthy opponent. I am startled by the scene laid out before me. She is someone of strength, and maybe even of substantial character, someone definitely not to be ignored.

I stand by the living room coffee table, staring down at a soiled deck of cards. Nurse Grace sits on the couch, her arms crossed, tapping one large foot on the carpeted floor. The glass table trembles at each thud, and I suddenly worry that it may crack right in two.

"Cards," she announces vehemently, as if in an argument with someone disputing what she has to say. "I just remembered that I had a pack in my purse and thought it would be fun to play."

But it is evident that fun is not what Nurse Grace is after now, her arms planted over her chest, her voice firm, resolute.

"Sit down, Noah, here on the couch beside me, or right there on the floor. Have you ever played War before? Do you know the rules of the game?"

I shrug, this form of body language now my favorite means of communication, and kneel right down in front of her dilapidated cards.

War, I think, *what an ironic name for a child's pastime*. Then I quickly remember the gift I had bought for myself on impulse the previous year, a game, yet challenging enough to pose Nurse Grace an interesting threat. It is clear that the woman is not well educated and has a vocabulary I have long surpassed. I point upstairs and then make a dignified exit. I march straight up to my room.

When I return, Nurse Grace has a blank expression on her face. Her arms are drooped over the white sofa cushions and she's leaning back as if to take a nap. As I enter the room, she sits up quickly and I cannot help but wonder what her reverie had been.

I unfold the game board carefully, setting the long, dark purple box cover aside. When I pull out the square wooden letters, Nurse Grace's eyes widen and she laughs.

"Scrabble!" she practically sings. "I've always wanted to learn how to play. My sixth-grade teacher told us that we could improve our vocabulary just by practicing, but my mother would never buy it for me, no matter what."

The corners of a few letter squares are rubbed off, so the varnish shines only in the center, some of the black alphabet imprints difficult to see. If it is a test of wits that she is after, I am definitely the one to take her on. Nurse Grace actually knows very little about me, or my accomplishments at school; she does not know that I read voraciously, way beyond my own grade level or maybe even her own adult capacity. She may throw down the gauntlet of a challenge, but I am certain to be more than capable with the written word.

I hand her the printed instructions and she nods, as if in agreement, then studies them over and over again. When she's ready, we both silently fill the small canvas bag with the smooth wooden letters.

I take the bundle in my hands and shake it. The squares click against each other like the chattering of teeth.

Nurse Grace counts out seven pieces, then turns each of them over.

I do the same.

She goes first. I'm not sure why, but I cannot

find a way to silently object.

Her word is silly, even infantile.

MOTHER

It seems that even Nurse Grace could do better than that. I hum to myself for a moment, then scan my letters for a vowel. It does not take me long. My word is perfect, in clear view, the last letter resting on one of the blue spots on the board indicating double credit. There is no question who will win.

MOAN

Nurse Grace doesn't flinch. She reaches into the bag for another letter, then studies it thoroughly, as if for clues. Once again her word is simple, even silly, easy to connect with something more substantial, something more complicated and worth additional points. More credit will soon be due me, and I resist the temptation to rub my hands together in delight. I will beat my alien intruder at this and every single other challenge, game, or test.

She sets down the wooden squares carefully, one by one, leaving her finger on the last for a long moment. She sighs and slides an *A* forward.

Ha, I think, *what could be easier?* Nurse Grace's word, attached to the *N* in *moan* has only three remaining letters, and I don't find this selection particularly appropriate to this game. Not at all.

NOAH

I think for a moment and then suddenly reconsider. Nurse Grace has committed a fatal error. It is spelled out in the directions, right there in the rules printed inside: you may never use a given name in Scrabble, you may never use anyone's name at all. And yet, as I chew on the corner of my cheek until it stings, I think maybe this is a trick, maybe she is just being clever. I will take my time before reacting, before rushing in too soon to make a much-regretted mistake.

After all, this is war.

Nurse Grace is tapping her fingers on the board as if impatient, as if anticipating my next move. If she thinks I will sink to her level, she is wrong. If she imagines that I will call her bluff, she is incorrect. Nurse Grace is trying to trick me into speaking with a vocal protestation of her breaking the rules of the game. But I am too smart for her, too astute. I will simply pretend not to notice and continue as before. I will set down one more word, just for emphasis, and then leave the room without waiting for anything more. There is, after all, no point in playing a game without any order—that makes no sense at all.

My last word is easy and automatically comes right to mind. Since Nurse Grace has spelled out *noah*, I attach three letters to the *h*. I tap the board for emphasis, and then turn away before it can be read.

HELP

"Noah," Nurse Grace calls after me, but soon I am already halfway up the stairs.

There are many ways to completely muffle all sounds of a gun, but the echo can always be heard.

I read in my room all morning, and surprisingly, I am left alone to my own devices. Expecting Nurse Grace to follow after me, for my doorknob to suddenly turn, for a knock or a call from the hall, I have one ear tuned in for oncoming footsteps. But all is quiet, not a single sound for several hours, not even from the other bedrooms or from the kitchen downstairs. Although it is a relief to be left to my own devices, somehow I find myself surprisingly fidgety, unable to completely relax or enjoy the book held up before my eyes. I am unusually distracted, unable to concentrate, and finally let the large volume slip from my hands to the floor.

Do I drift off to sleep for a few moments? I'm not sure.

I hear someone crying out in distress—am I dreaming or does the phone ring, are there footsteps running? Does something crash and fall?

I sit up suddenly, thinking of Mademoiselle, and look at the clock. It is already noon. I must have fallen asleep without even realizing it; an hour or so has passed without my being aware. I hold my breath and listen, but there is no sound or movement anywhere at all.

By 12:30 I realize I am surprisingly hungry, that my stomach is uncharacteristically growling, waiting to be filled. I stand and stretch, then notice an aroma drifting through the door. A scent rich with complexity, somewhat spicy, yet mild at the same time. Perhaps I can ignore it and maintain my dignity by remaining alone in my room. Maybe I will resist giving in, preserving my isolation, remaining hungry, upstairs, with no one to tell me what to do or what I should be eating. But soon I find myself walking hesitantly to my door and then opening it slowly.

The fragrance billows up into my face, beckoning, and I am suddenly starving. I cannot remember ever being this ravenous, and before I even know what I am doing, I find myself moving forward without thinking, as if in a trance. I am walking almost unconsciously, straight down the stairs.

There is a rustle in the kitchen, and I inhale the aroma as it intensifies, my feet picking up speed. But as I pass the living room table, I notice the Scrabble board has not been removed. For some reason, despite myself, I stop to examine the pattern of letters, and am not at all surprised to see a new word. Nurse Grace has been hard at work, I whisper to myself, but I will not be deterred. It appears that her new word is a bit more ambitious this time, longer, with additional vowels.

LISTEN

My heart floods with anger, and the blood rushes to my head. This woman, this alien invader, is insatiable; she will not give up without devouring me whole. No, I will not acknowledge her message, nor will I be forced into listening at all. Nurse Grace must make do if she is to stay here and learn to leave me to my own private world. I will not be hounded by a stranger; I will not disclose what she wants so desperately to know.

Her word, spelled out on the game board, will not have the desired or adequate response. This nurse is in my employment, hardly a mother whose oxygen once provided her child air. In fact, she is nothing more than a charlatan, simply a caretaker who is no blood relation at all. What gives her the right to chase after me, demanding this or that? I will retreat with silence if I have to, and she will not have any power to object.

No wonder I think about my double, the

other half of my embittered core. No wonder I must fight to protect his identity, no wonder speech is no longer a choice. Nurse Grace, and who knows who else, will not give up until I break. They will never leave me alone; they will shadow me forever, insisting that I reveal all.

But my twin's rage is relentless, unmerciful, and he speaks out for me when I am silent, when I don't have the same inclination or will.

It is both frightening and reassuring to imagine him out there wandering, scaling the edge of this lonely world. He casts his monstrous fury forward, hook, line, and sinker, finding revenge in a tangled net.

I am small and I am feeble, half a boy without any words, but my shadow is a changeling, mercurial, invulnerable, quick to disappear.

I will never betray him, no matter what harm he has done. I will forever conceal his identity, I will never give him up.

My silence protects us both, a shield safeguarding twin souls.

I think for a moment, determined not to be overtaken. It takes only a minute to respond to

Nurse Grace's scrabbled message and I fit one letter neatly underneath the *N* of my name: *O*.

N O

I turn to admire the result, and smile. My word may not garner many points—it does not even find itself on a double-credit blue square—but its meaning is evident.

There can be no misunderstanding; my position is made perfectly clear.

The bullet penetrates deeply, often causing shock and terrible damage.

Nurse Grace barely looks up as I join her at the kitchen table, and passes me a bowl of thick vegetable stew.

We bend over our food together, two grim faces moistened with steam, mouths wide open, both stomachs desperate to be fed.

GRACE

The boy's stopped speaking, and Grace immediately wonders what she's done wrong.

She's certain that Noah's silence is her fault.

And the day had begun so well. Grace made Noah baked apples for breakfast, a meal chockfull of the vitamins he so badly needs, and it actually thrilled her to see him have two servings, to watch him enjoy the warm food on his plate. So at first, she thinks Noah's silence is a result of his concentration on the food, his savoring of each and every bite. It isn't until much later that she realizes something else is afoot.

In any case, the morning meal is a pleasure and Grace actually feels a sense of accomplishment watching the boy eat so well. Such an easy dish to make, this recipe, a mainstay of her own early childhood, and she remembers cold, snowy days punctuated with the warmth of her grandmother's hot MacIntosh apples coated with sugar and cream. Although her mother's mother used to visit frequently, somehow those occasions suddenly stopped after Liam's death. And then her grandmother had, to everyone's surprise, remarried and was living across the country, in Arizona.

"Thank God she's no longer my responsibility," Grace's mother had said to her once, sitting on the worn brown velveteen living room couch and rubbing her feet with both hands. "At least I know that she's taken care of and I don't have to worry."

The comment had surprised Grace, and it occurred to her how easy it was for someone to disappear. Suddenly out of sight and out of mind. She had shivered then and bowed her head so that her mother would not see her eyes fill up hot.

As time passed, Grace's mother's contact with her own mother lessened and then finally ground to a halt, until they barely wrote or telephoned each other at all. Yes, there was the distance to consider now, and the expense of airfare, as well as the time required to travel so far, but one would think that none of this would keep a mother and child apart.

Can that happen? Grace wonders as she watches Noah eat his food—is it possible to stop being a mother once your life changes, is it possible for a child to suddenly vanish from your memory at the drop of a hat? How can a parent turn her back when her own child is in need, no matter what the situation, no matter the demands of a new family or of a different home? How could a mother possibly begin to forget?

Even in death, Grace hasn't abandoned Liam; he's with her now, as he is every minute of every single day.

Well, Grace thinks, *you can't assume that everyone will rally in a crisis, no matter what's expected*. When Liam was killed, she watched her own closest friends retreating, practically seeing the very whites of their terrified eyes. The kindest of faces suddenly hardened, their expressions turning frightened and stern, and their conversations becoming tentative, somehow muffled and difficult to understand. It was as if, all at once, activity around Grace deteriorated into slow motion and she was submerged somewhere underwater, trying desperately to find her way to the top. But try as she might, all she saw were ghostly faces at the surface, blurry reflections in a bottomless lake, words spoken but distorted by watery distance.

Grace's Death Card was inverted, upside down. Stagnation, inertia, immobility. No possibility of change. She knew this, but couldn't find a way to make a reversal.

Eventually she stopped trying. She realized that it wasn't only Liam's death that sent her plunging beneath, but her own inability to stroke upward again and to inhale. The world, for her, was forever poisoned with tragedy and flooded with grief. Ordinary humans walking the globe seemed suddenly alien, horrifying in their hideous lack of grace.

So now, when Noah draws back silent, when she recognizes a similar fear reflected in his eyes, Grace realizes that she herself has become the outsider, an intruder in his own private world, and this makes her sad. The strange thing is that she feels somehow angry, frustrated, and irritated with the boy. She realizes that these feelings are unfounded; Noah is simply unable to control his actions or emotions during this difficult period in his life. But when he opts for complete silence, refusing to speak a single word, she interprets his rejection as personal. She feels painfully responsible for this turn of events, but doesn't know how or why. And anger creeps into her body, surprising her with its pressing need to be heard.

Something about Noah's stubborn silence provokes Grace, making her feel all the more determined to communicate with this lonely, forgotten boy. She begins to notice in herself a long-lost emotion, something akin to energy, spirit, drive, obstinate pride. She won't accept Noah's rejection and must do everything in her power to bring him back to life. She will not be waylaid.

The rules of the tarot are clear: listen to yourself, use your intuition, follow your heart.

When Noah stays in his room all afternoon,

Grace becomes aware that she could use a rest herself and considers lying down for a nap. But there's no time for a break, and she forces herself to start on some of the cleaning that she's put off for so long. After taking a deep breath, she heads toward the grandmother's dark room and, worried about making a disturbance, tiptoes quietly inside. She stops suddenly, midstride, hearing something rustle, but quickly realizes that it's simply a blanket that's slipped from the old woman's bed to the floor. Carefully, slowly, she makes her way across the room, takes another deep breath, and replaces the quilt on the foot of the bed, making sure that it drapes neatly over both sides and retucking the loose corners. All is perfectly quiet except for the low, shaky hum of her own breathing—all perfectly still. She reminds herself to empty the dusty glass of water on the tray left by the tufted satin ottoman, then stands still by the grandmother's bed, inhaling the sour, musty odor of the very old.

Why would a woman of this age put herself and her grandson through such an ordeal? Grace wonders. Where is the logic in that? Why take this kind of risk simply for a superficial result?

The white wicker hamper by the bathroom is half open, and Grace bends to collect a mound of ivory silk sheets in her arms, then tiptoes out again, equally careful not to disturb. As she slowly closes the door behind her, she thinks she hears a window slam shut, but when she pokes her head back inside, all is quiet. Grace shivers, clutching the linens to her chest; sometimes, she thinks, this job is simply too upsetting, too unnerving to bear, and is suddenly surprised by her own squeamishness. "Not very professional," Mrs. Saville would say. "Not very professional at all."

She spends much of the afternoon finishing the cooking of dinner, something begun earlier in the morning, cutting up the raw chicken carcass, then rinsing the poultry in the sink and patting it dry with paper towels, as her mother had taught her many years ago. She realizes, however, that another batch must be made so that there will be enough food for dinner and lunch the next day. The uncooked flesh feels slick to her touch, rubbery and cold, almost repellent, and she's relieved to finally line up the pink pieces neatly in a rectangular glass pan. The meat roasts slowly, uncovered for thirty minutes, and then is sprinkled with dried apricots and currants that have marinated in orange juice sweetened with unprocessed brown sugar. Twenty minutes more and the second dish is ready; all she has left is the simmering of brown rice and the steaming of broccoli, the perfect addition to this particular recipe, hopefully to be accepted by the boy.

As she slides the pan of chicken out of the oven, she notices a stinging on her right hand, and then sees a trickle of blood from her palm to her wrist. The oven door slams quickly, as if on its own, and Grace sees that she's cut her index finger. It's quite an impressive slice. She must have nicked it while chopping vegetables, something that's happened before.

After wrapping her finger tightly with a paper towel and rushing upstairs, Grace rummages through the small linen closet in the hallway, a narrow corner cupboard built into the wall. There's a pile of pale towels neatly folded side by side, a large humidifier still in its broad cardboard box, a white silk blanket covered in thick plastic wrap, and a small shoe box filled with two large bottles of mouthwash, five unused toothbrushes, iodine, cough medicine—clearly unopened and also in the original container. Grace looks closer and is pleased to see a small container of Band-Aids neatly tucked away to one side, but when she reaches for it, she shrieks and drops it to the floor. The bottom of the box is crawling with black insects: hideous, long, and furry, some kind of enormous cockroach or water bug. Dark and coarse haired—disgusting. She hears herself gasp and stumbles backward. But when she tentatively leans forward again, her fingers slipping on the wall as she tries to hold on, Grace sees that the bugs are not actually crawling, not actually moving at all. Just a tangle of matted black tentacles, squashed wings, flattened bodies, perhaps all dead, smothered together in the shoe box for who knows how long, decomposing, one on top of the other, stuck in a jumbled mess.

Grace thinks she might be sick.

The Band-Aids have spilled out all over the floor, and as she takes a tentative step forward to retrieve several with one hand, she tries to shove the shoe box back into the closet without looking inside. Stuck. She starts to jiggle it while keeping a safe distance away, and a bug drops down by her left foot. She jumps. Its tentacles fan out like a tuft of human hair, and suddenly Grace sees that it isn't an insect at all. She smiles to herself and then chuckles, sliding slowly to the floor. The dark dot by her shoe is a false eyelash, a tiny synthetic strip of fake hair and nothing more. It lies there on the carpet, one edge dotted with dried white glue, and when she taps it with one finger, it sticks to her flesh, a black butterfly hovering on the branch of a human tree.

Grace shudders despite herself and stands up slowly. She shoves the box back onto its shelf, gathers the loose Band-Aids into her hand, wrapping one quickly around her finger, and then closes the closet door. Fake eyelashes, nothing alive, nothing to harm her, yet she feels unsettled, unnerved. "Get a grip," Grace mutters to herself. "Get a grip, girl, or you won't last another day."

There's no conversation at dinner, as expected, Noah accepting his food but still unwilling to speak. He chews slowly, spearing tiny pieces, never looking up or taking his eyes from his meal, scraping the plate before him with fork tines until the painful sound makes Grace shiver.

At first she tries to match his silence with her own, but eventually finds herself chatting away as if nothing's unusual. It's as though she can't help breaking the tension, feeling the silent gulf between them widening without the bridging of words, and she's frightened that there won't be an end to this distance as it grows larger and larger. So, as she talks to him as though nothing is different, as though it's a normal dinner held during normal circumstances—simply routine— at the same time, she is all at once thinking of how to handle the future, how to approach this challenging situation during the long days of the week to come.

As Grace chews her chicken thoughtfully,

and speaks to Noah about the meaningless events of her day, she is surreptitiously thinking of something else—she's hatching a secret plan of attack in her head.

· DAY SIX ·

GRACE

The idea comes to her suddenly. Maybe just a little bit silly, but Grace doesn't know why she hasn't thought of it before. After all, if the boy doesn't want to talk, he doesn't have to. She'll find another way to keep him company without his having to say a word. But, of course, when she offers to play cards with him, having remembered the old pack in her purse, he just smirks and shakes his head. And before Grace knows it, he has disappeared upstairs. But this time, to her surprise, before long Noah returns with a box, the game of Scrabble, something she has never learned. Well, okay, she should let him take charge when possible, give in to his wishes whenever she can, at least let him have some control over his life, even if it's only a game.

But before they're finished playing, once

again Noah suddenly vanishes, leaving her with nothing to do but stare into space and think about the meaning of the last word formed with the small wooden squares.

HELP.

If only she knew how. If only he'd tell her what he needs and what he's feeling.

Oh, well, just like yesterday, she'll let the boy have his peace for a while, give him a little space, before overwhelming him once more with her concern and her words. She'll spend the afternoon preparing his dinner, chopping up vegetables, concocting the most nutritious and delectable of stews. Carrots, onions, green beans, and peppers. Spinach, squash, and red potatoes. Asparagus, broccoli, and sweet corn. What could be better, more nutritious for a boy half grown?

Grace searches the kitchen cabinets, looking for a pot large enough to accommodate the colorful collection of vegetables, but sees only one tiny sauté pan and the two pathetically small kettles she found the first day. It's as if this is a house with a play kitchen—only a few dishes, several pieces of clearly unused silverware, and three small cooking utensils that are miniature compared to what she has at home.

How did the grandmother manage, Grace asks herself, stretching her arm up to the farthest cupboard, hidden above the oven hood, barely within her reach. How on earth did Noah's Mademoiselle care for her grandson, with no food or cooking utensils to be found anywhere?

The cabinet door is stuck as if locked. Grace has to twist the handle with all her force, and she stumbles backward when it finally pops ajar.

Her mouth drops open in amazement as she looks at what is concealed within. She blinks, and then stares inside again.

The narrow cupboard is filled with empty glass bottles, practically stuffed to capacity, and it's immediately clear what they once contained. Grace steps closer to the open shelf and reaches up again to pull one down, the label pasted on the diagonal, the lettering black: JOHNNIE WALKER RED, she reads, and then looks up again. The next bottle is taller: TWELVE-YEAR-OLD SINGLE MALT—DOUBLE WOOD. Grace idly wonders what "double wood" means, and then turns to another bottle, this one a poisonous dark green. The word *Chartreuse* is spelled out in gold print, and since she has never heard of such a drink, Grace studies the list of ingredients on the back with interest: elixir, Vegetable, alcohol, plants, flowers. She can't resist smiling to herself; at least it does not include the dread processed ingredients or saturated fat. The next bottle is rum, still emanating a ripe, sickly-sweet odor, and the next another whisky, then sherry, vodka, tonic, and then sherry again.

Grace pulls out a chair from the nearby table and slowly sits down. She doesn't have any desire to look at the rest of the bottles crammed together on the crowded shelf; there are too many, and anyway, she already knows what will be found.

So the old woman had a problem, Grace thinks, maybe even an addiction—it's really hard to know.

Surely the boy hasn't been filling this high cupboard with empty liquor bottles. Certainly Noah hasn't been consuming whisky and sherry and god knows what else.

No wonder the kitchen is empty and the boy

is underfed. Like Grace's own mother, the old woman had a fondness for the bottle, clearly forgetting what it means to raise a child. For a minute Grace feels her heart racing, and takes a deep breath. A boy raised in a house with a neglectful guardian, clearly unable to meet her grandchild's basic needs. How long has this gone on, she wonders. It all makes sense to her now: the empty house, the lack of food, the boy's frail body and pale complexion, his hesitancy to eat.

Grace looks at the bottles in her hands and decides what she must do. She'll put them back in the cupboard for now, and turn back to making dinner, finishing the vegetable stew. Some other time in the future, another afternoon when the boy's sure to be otherwise occupied, Grace will gather the liquor bottles in a large cardboard box. She'll haul them out to the garbage and close the container lid tightly.

She'll never tell any of this to Noah. He'll never have to know.

When the phone rings later, Grace is startled, concentrating on slicing the yellow summer squash into circles, and careful to avoid cutting herself in the process. She even jumps at the harsh chiming, a sudden interruption of the house's complete silence with which she has become so familiar.

Her first thought is of upstairs, that the ringing phone will cause alarm or interrupt the much-needed rest. And then it occurs to her. The call may be for Grace herself, it may be just the news she has been awaiting so long. She puts the knife down carefully and watches a small red potato roll from the counter onto the floor. She doesn't bend down to pick it up. She's all at once frozen, unable to move.

The phone rings again and she suddenly springs into motion, rushing up the stairs, grabbing at the instrument with both hands and knocking the metal stand completely over on one side. She pulls the cord into her bedroom and hurries to close the door.

"Yes," she practically shouts breathlessly. "Yes, I'm here, hello, this is the Ships' residence. Grace Rush speaking."

"Mrs. Rush?"

Grace can hardly believe it. She immediately

recognizes the deep voice, its hesitation.

"Miss, not Mrs. Yes, this is Grace Rush."

"Detective Hinkle here. Sorry it took so long to get back to you—I planned to call you again right away that very afternoon. Do you remember me? I believe we spoke just the other day."

She bends over at the waist for a moment, feeling light-headed, even a bit faint, and then straightens up, preparing herself for what must eventually be heard. Finally, after all this time, she's to learn what actually happened and who was responsible.

"Hello, Detective Hinkle." Her voice is surprisingly collected. "Of course I remember. Thank you for calling back. I appreciate it. You can't imagine how long I have waited to be told. I realize you may not have all the answers, but anything at all would help."

"Well, please don't thank me yet." The detective's voice wavers for a moment and Grace's blood runs cold. "I'm afraid I may not have the exact information you are looking for, but I have come across something that may be helpful and that should bring you some comfort."

Grace squeezes the cord around her fingers until they hurt. She looks at the red mark on her skin and then hangs her head down.

"Mrs. . . . Miss Rush?"

"Yes, I'm still here."

"As I was saying, I know that you are eager to identify the perpetrator, and we at the station are always interested in solving a terrible case such as this. But I'm afraid that with all the recent shootings—maybe I shouldn't even be telling you this, but just the same—with all the demands of the sniper case, we're all spread pretty thin. I wasn't able to find anyone who originally worked on your brother's case to be available. In fact, it is almost impossible to run down any significant information at all."

So why are you calling, Grace thinks, her mouth filling up with bitterness, her heart so heavy that she thinks it might drop down all the way to her toes. *Why call me at all, you stupid idiot, just go back to your cage and leave me alone.* But of course she says nothing close to this, shutting her eyes and inhaling deeply. She has no intention of completely severing her relationship with the police. Not just now. Not when there are still answers to be found.

"Anyway . . ."

Is the detective still speaking? Somehow Grace thought he'd hung up the phone.

"Anyway," he continues slowly, "although I was not able to find out anything about the accident itself, I'm able to tell you about something else that should be meaningful, something important that you definitely should know."

Grace can't imagine what this could be or what the word *meaningful* could possibly convey. Unless Liam has been found out there somewhere, alive and waiting to return home, unless his mutilated four-year-old little body has been pieced back together seamlessly, unless the scrabble of his corpse has been reconfigured, unless pure, sweet breath has been funneled back within . . .

"While looking through the files, I found that the recipient family has been trying to contact you and your mother. It's the donation that I am referring to." His voice begins to weaken; is it her imagination or has the detective somehow materialized right here in the room with her, whispering rank breath in her ear, telling her ugly secrets that she would rather have left unknown? "The organ donation, Miss Rush. I found some paperwork on the proceedings and a name and an address. I believe I have located information relative to the recipient of your brother's heart. Apparently the parents have been trying to contact you for quite a while."

Liam's small organs had been donated.

"So someone else might live," the doctor had said. "Perhaps even another child."

But Grace did not want other children living, she wanted Liam back, she wanted him intact and alive, she wanted him whole.

Liver, kidneys, and heart.

How she railed against any intrusion, any separation of what was once complete, yelling and pleading day after day in a rant against donation, eventually even furiously throwing her pocketbook at the wall. But her mother eventually agreed with the doctor, too tired to argue, too numb to disagree with what was recommended. Grace remembers how her mother tried to take her arm that final moment, how she slowly whispered into the poisonous hospital air, "Let's just get out of here, Gracie. I don't care, I don't care, I just don't care anymore. What the doctors say makes sense, maybe some other kid can be helped. I don't know. I just want to go home and as far away from this hospital as I possibly can."

Grace would fume in her bed at night, her heart clenched like a fist, exhausted but unable to sleep, and she would shrink from the comfort of her own sheets.

Night after night, Grace would close her eyes and pretend to drowse.

But all she could see was Liam's miniature corpse, carved out hollow, curled stiff underground.

Shut up, she hears herself scream silently into the phone, *stop, shut up, shut up, shut up right now.*

Her head is spinning, her heart thudding, and all of her own huge, bloated organs float up suddenly before her. She watches them hover there, crudely misshapen, hideously bruised and blackened, and then the bare arms of the great bloody vessels looming above, the aorta and vena cava, exposed, pulsing wildly out of control.

Her chest is split wide open, the danger imminent, no known cure for the trauma of such a penetrating, internal wound.

Future life may be impossible.

Grace feels her body scraped empty, nothing left in the deep cavity inside, and she can almost smell the raw, meaty odor of her internal organs, she can smell them rotting out in the open air.

"Detective," she says evenly, nauseated and surprised at the composure of her own hard little voice, "I am not able to talk anymore right now." And then she clicks on the telephone receiver twice to make sure that the disconnect is complete, and winds the cord into three neat circles. She opens her bedroom door, returns the receiver to its rightful place, steadies the telephone stand, and adjusts her posture until her shoulders are completely straight.

She has dinner to make, hasn't she? She has an important job to complete.

What gives this man, this detective, the right to judge what is meaningful, what might be a comfort to her, what is important—what gives him the right to judge anything at all?

Why does he think he can unnerve her with

his dirty secrets and unwanted words?

She will forget everything that has been said.

In fact, she will forget that this call has ever even been made.

·DAY SEVEN·

NOAH

No shootings are reported today, nor any apprehension of suspects.

The front page of the morning newspaper includes a large photograph of the Geneva County chief of police, with a caption underneath: *Chief Albert Ridel Angered by Leak to Press in Sniper Probe.*

I stare at the picture for a minute. The chief's expression is anguished and his face is contorted; it almost looks as though the tall, gray-haired man is about to cry.

That couldn't be right. A chief of police, a man of this stature and of his age, simply does not break down in tears.

I look to my left to read the full article, but, of course, my concentration is broken as

Nurse Grace interrupts.

"Did you look at the paper yet, Noah? Did you read that several other tarot cards were found at the scene of the last two shootings, but Chief Ridel hadn't wanted this reported? It says right here in this morning's newspaper that this information shouldn't have been leaked to the press but that some thoughtless reporter got wind of the cards having been discovered at the crime scenes, and now it's all over the press."

I shake my head, my eyes glued to the newsprint in an effort to communicate that I am interested in reading the paper myself. Of course, Nurse Grace neglects to interpret my cues and continues talking while she spreads what looks to be pale apple butter on two pieces of whole wheat toast.

"It's an interesting predicament, isn't it," she says, almost to herself, "between the media's obligation to report all information to the public and the police's need to keep certain things secret. When to speak out and when to keep quiet. I'm not quite sure where I stand on this subject. While I certainly want the murderer caught, and caught right away, I'm not sure that the withholding of newsworthy details from the community is such a good thing. And look what happens, anyway. Eventually, in this kind of a situation, there is usually some kind of leak. It's almost impossible to keep some things hidden, underground, for long, when everyone is so scared. Knowledge can be dangerous sometimes—it's often better not to know each and every last detail, but the truth eventually seems to come out, no matter what. Don't you think? How do you feel about all of this, Noah?"

I roll my eyes, my face hidden by the newspaper held in front of my face. I am certainly not interested in being impolite to Nurse Grace, but she knows perfectly well that I have no intention of responding.

"Oh, for a minute I forgot that you're not speaking to me anymore. How silly of me to expect that you've changed your mind overnight."

Again the sarcasm in her voice.

"Well," she continues, sliding the plate of buttered toast across the table so that it stops directly in front of me, shuddering in a golden glow. "I guess I'll just have to talk to myself. It's clear that you aren't going to show me the courtesy of responding."

Am I jumping to conclusions or is something different about Nurse Grace this morning? Her voice seems surprisingly harsh, and her words, usually carefully chosen and spoken gently with care, seem clipped, provocative, even a bit unpleasant.

I lower the paper discreetly and try to peer at her without being noticed. She is standing at the sink, her back facing me, and she rubs the nape of her neck with one hand as if in pain. Then, for or a minute or two, Nurse Grace is perfectly immobile, frozen. She remains completely still without moving a muscle, then suddenly sighs to herself and resumes wiping the counter with her favorite soiled sponge.

I look down at the toast in front of me and, to my very own surprise, find myself wishing for a larger breakfast, for Nurse Grace's usual hot morning meal. The toast, while not unappealing, does not seem adequate for my appetite today, and I wonder why such a slight breakfast this morning. Is my provider upset with me, is she communicating her disappointment with a paltry offering of food? I look over at Nurse Grace again. She is staring at the wall, and although I cannot see her face, I somehow can imagine the rigid set of her jaw, the furrow in her brow.

Has my silence caused this shift in personality? Has my decision to remain mute resulted in this usually cheerful woman's sudden black mood?

I find myself tempted to say something aloud, to ask her what's wrong, if I am the reason for her irritable state of mind or if something else is responsible. I open my mouth but immediately close it again. I resist the impulse to speak.

Enter the quiet world of silencers.

She spins around suddenly and continues her prattle as if the original monologue had never been interrupted.

"It's the tarot cards that I find intriguing." She speaks quickly, in an even, calmer tone, and begins piling dishes in the sink. "It seems to me that it's got to be a pretty educated person who would use the tarot to leave messages. Not just anybody is into the psychic world."

My appetite for breakfast, enormous just a few minutes ago, suddenly dwindles. In fact, I don't think I will be able to eat anything at all.

Nurse Grace stops talking for a moment and I can feel her eyes upon me. Then, without warning, she continues. "It's almost more frightening, isn't it, to think that someone of a similar background, maybe from our own neighborhood, someone just like you and me, someone who may look just like us, but whose heart must be thoroughly cold, could be out there wreaking such havoc, creating such pain for so many. I think it would be less terrifying if the shooter was some kind of raving lunatic escaped from an institution, a monster who isn't even human, something completely alien, grotesque, unrecognizable to any of us at all. But," she continues despite the fact that I do not move the paper from my face, "from all the evidence, it appears that he looks quite ordinary. The murderer apparently looks just like any normal boy or young man. Why, the eyewitness accounts describe someone who could be living right next door—his appearance is unremarkable, nothing unusual, slim and small in stature. As a matter of fact, the descriptions even match your general appearance."

Despite myself, I put the paper down on the table next to the uneaten toast.

My whole body freezes and I suddenly understand the meaning of the expression "blood running cold." It is a perfect description of my condition at that very moment. My hands begin to shake, mildly at first, as if from the inside out, then more and more all over again.

"Noah?"

Nurse Grace's voice is clear. I can understand each and every word spoken, but for some reason it seems to drift into the house from outside. I hear her speaking, but her words sound faraway, more of an echoing than an actual human voice.

"Noah, are you all right? You look awfully pale."

I inhale and shake my head.

The bullet makes a much smaller hole when it enters the body than when it exits.

"Here, drink something. A sip of juice."

She hands me a glass of orange juice and holds it under my mouth.

My lips are pressed so tightly together that I cannot budge them open, no matter how hard I try. In fact, for a minute I am not able to move any muscle, big or small.

It is as if, for this single minute, my body is no longer under my own control, inhabited suddenly by someone else's soul.

Nurse Grace doesn't say anything, and in fact, she seems to disappear out of sight; has she left the room without making a sound, or has she simply vanished into thin air? Is it possible for such a large woman to evaporate without a trace? Somehow I am unable to move my head or look around.

Suddenly, a rustle from behind, and I feel something nudge me on the back, the insistent pawing of a huge, unfamiliar creature.

I hold my breath. I will not turn around. The

hairs on my arms do not stand up. They sink. They pierce hundreds of tiny paths, cold needles underneath my skin.

My chair is sliding, the floor drops, the air solidifies and then cracks into jagged chunks of ice.

"Noah?"

The voice is familiar, but I cannot see the face.

And then I realize, of course, it is only Nurse Grace standing behind me, it is only her hand patting me gently on the back. The warmth of her flesh seeps through my shirt and the outline of each finger on my skin burns. If I were to look at my unclothed back in the mirror, there would be an imprint of Nurse Grace's large, capable, unflinching hand.

All at once, I feel my body come back to life and the blood within stir. Somehow a drop of juice finds its way to my dry tongue, and then another. Before I know it, I am drinking down the sweet liquid in large gulps.

"There." Nurse Grace exhales as if relieved and then sits down next to me. "I think that you may be just a bit dehydrated. For a moment, Noah, you gave me quite a scare, and I thought you might keel over in a dead faint. Here, have another glass. You've got to make sure to drink enough liquids if you want to stay healthy. I'll make sure to get another quart of juice later today at the store."

My eyes remain lowered. I refuse to meet her look, but continue sipping from the glass as if I had not had anything to drink for days.

"I really hope that you're not becoming ill, Noah," she says quietly. "That's all you need right now. It could be everything that's happened: your grandmother, and then this nasty business of the sniper; well, it may just be too much for someone of your age. It's no wonder that you're kind of beat. Why don't you just take it easy today and I'll whip up another breakfast for you right now. It's clear that this toast doesn't make the grade— you haven't had a bite—and, anyway, toast really isn't much of a meal, is it? I really don't know what came over me this morning, why I didn't cook something heartier for my growing boy. Here, let me take this away and find you something heartier. After all, that's why I'm here in the first place, isn't it? To take care? I'm sorry, Noah, for a minute I seemed to have forgotten my job, my position here, and unfortunately got caught up in my own personal worries."

She shakes her head as if exasperated, and then sighs.

It is hard not to wonder what Nurse Grace's personal worries might be.

Somehow, I have never thought of her in this way, as an actual human being with her own separate sorrows, wishes, and desires. All of a sudden, I am curious about Nurse Grace's life outside of this house, and wonder what her own home is like, where she lives, who her friends are, what she does for pleasure and for fun.

I watch this large young woman as she bustles around the small kitchen, snatching things from the refrigerator and tossing them into a steaming pan of what looks like real dairy butter. But I'm somehow suddenly exhausted, too tired to object, as if it were late in the evening instead of first thing in the morning. I sit back lazily in my chair, listening to the sound of rich ingredients fill the small pan like children's chatter. I close my eyes.

Nurse Grace has called me "her" boy and I am not even disturbed. She is cooking a meal filled with saturated fats and grams and grams of forbidden cholesterol and I don't seem to care.

My stomach is empty, but I know that it will soon be filled.

There's clearly something satisfying in the experience of hunger while just about to be fed.

For some reason, and to my very own surprise, I find myself wanting to remain in this very chair in the safety of this very kitchen for a long time to come. In this moment, there is nowhere else I would rather be.

The small room is warming up quickly and Nurse Grace is humming a tune I find familiar, a childhood lyric that I think I may have heard sung to me a long, long time ago.

Something about being lost.

Something about being found.

"I'm curious about all of your books, Noah," Nurse Grace says after I have finished eating. She has washed all the dishes, and turns to look at me, hands at her hips.

She seems calmer now, as if feeding me a hot breakfast has soothed her raw nerves, and I wonder how she knows about my reading and collection of literature. I know that she has been in my room on several occasions, but never considered that she might notice anything about my surroundings.

"I admire someone who reads so much, can find such pleasure in the written word. For me, I just don't seem to have the patience."

I smile despite myself.

What does patience have to do with it?

How can pleasure not be found?

The secret life of words, of books.

Reading is my sixth sense.

Sometimes I am amazed how black curls on an ordinary piece of paper can become selves, whole lives, worlds. How the one-dimensional becomes two.

Books are beautiful to me, their stiff bindings, their musty scent, the heavy cream-colored pages, the engraved title. The page and I exchange the sweetest of whimpers, so small, so infinitesimal a motion, that the mouth barely moves at all, and I am immediately transported elsewhere, a fortunate boy, all by myself.

I have often seen Mademoiselle experiencing something similar, when she is savoring her evening drink. My grandmother would suddenly leave me, although remaining right by my side. All of a sudden, the fragrance of Mademoiselle's sherry drifts up under my nose and I close my eyes. Time collapses and I am no longer where I am.

I am four years old again and Mademoiselle is bending down over me. Her breath is amber, liquid and sweet. Like cough syrup. Like the thick potion that slithers down your throat when you are ill. You will not forget its taste, you will not forget its smell.

Mademoiselle and I are standing outside the house.

The top snap on her blouse glitters like the gold tooth in the back of a gaping mouth, and the hem of her burgundy dress rubs against her heavy silk hose.

I can see a tuft of bleached hair over her painted lips.

"Child," she whispers right into my little face, "your shoes are filthy. Did I not tell you to leave those old things at home and wear the new oxfords I had sent over from the store? You know, my dear, if you intend to remain here with me, you must learn to listen and behave. Do remember this: You are a lucky boy to have a place to stay, considering the circumstances. Now, let's go inside, my darling, and we will overlook this unfortunate event."

Mademoiselle straightens up, takes a step back, and then looks me all over from top to bottom. She shakes her head. And then she walks away, leaving me alone on the curb in front of her little brick house, a trail of bitter words filling up my fresh, young air.

I am standing in the kitchen now, grown to a full thirteen years old, an entire nine years later. I am washing the water glasses, listening to Nurse Grace's chatter, and that one single, imaginary whiff of sherry brings Mademoiselle back to my side, as if she had never gone.

·DAY SEVEN·

GRACE

The boy worries her so.

His thin, pointed face.

His sour expression. His nervousness.

His silence.

His fragility.

His moments of sudden alarm.

It's strange that he so rarely asks about his grandmother, about what's to happen next, how he'll cope after Grace's temporary placement is over. What's still to be done, who will take on her duties, how Noah will manage with a new adult in charge? Thank goodness Mrs. Saville has approved her remaining another week; Grace cannot imagine leaving yet. No one would be prepared for such a separation—and she hasn't even had the opportunity to really talk to

Noah about his feelings or encourage him to express his anxiety and sorrow.

Just this morning, Grace sees Noah go white for no apparent reason, as if he's glimpsed a ghost of some kind. And she can't figure out what causes this sudden, dramatic change in demeanor, although, of course, she realizes that the loss of the grandmother's everyday presence in his life must be overwhelming, and this business with the shootings couldn't be helping much at all.

In fact, anybody of any age would find it challenging to cope with the concept of a faceless murderer crouching somewhere out there, just waiting for another victim to appear. Perhaps she shouldn't continue to talk about the shootings so frequently, maybe all of the details are too upsetting for a boy of Noah's age. Sometimes, in bed late at night, Grace finds herself thinking about the sniper and her eyes will open wide, as if an intruder had suddenly entered her room, making it difficult to breathe, every shadow poised for attack, every sound full of meaning. She'll feel like a little child then, her own blood gone gummy with fear, her tongue swollen, the moon leering through her window, an enormous beam aimed directly on her face. Grace will feel her mattress slowly rise like her brother's small hospital bed, cranked higher and higher, a tiny figure helpless against what is to come, a giant hand offering them both up to who knows what.

When the doctor bent to examine him that last time.

When the two nurses exchanged glances.

When she struggled to stand up and plead.

When there was nothing but the sound of the drip.

The medicine, the machine.

Then nothing at all.

Just before the decision was made to let him go. Only one day until.

Just before that.

At dinner, Grace doesn't even attempt a conversation with the boy. She's somehow worn out, and content to sit with him over the evening meal and appreciate the silence. Noah may not feel like talking, but Grace finds that she doesn't mind and is no longer irritated or resentful. She feels a sudden affection for this odd, somber child, and watches him carefully as he slowly eats his food, putting off her other duties and obligations for a short while.

Noah meticulously cuts his pot roast into small pieces and then chews each one as if savoring each and every bite. Then he turns to the remaining mashed potatoes, stirs them with a fork into a peaked swirl. Grace tries not to chuckle as he drops a large cube of butter in the middle of his plate and then drowns the potatoes in the melting oil. By the time he's finished, the boy's mouth is shining as if polished and he wears the contented expression of someone well fed.

Well, Grace thinks, she's obviously doing something right. She's managed to turn this part of Noah's life around.

Perhaps, for now, that is enough. Perhaps she will not ask for anything more.

WEEK TWO

THE MOON

The moon pours its light into our hearts, overwhelming reason
and illuminating our impulsive nature.

I rush downstairs to breakfast, eager to read the news of the day and see what Nurse Grace has prepared for this morning's meal. But there are no odors of anything being cooked, no sounds from the kitchen below.

I stop and listen.

My stomach growls and I recognize hunger.

Just as I am almost all the way to the bottom of the stairs, however, I hear unfamiliar voices. At first I am unable to locate the source, and close my eyes as if to sharpen the senses. Is it the television, the radio, or am I actually overhearing the conversation of human voices? Perhaps someone unfamiliar unexpectedly entered my home, became involved in a discussion with Nurse Grace. I turn completely around and hurry back up the stairs, then wait, listening nervously from the front bedroom hall.

The unidentifiable sound continues, even louder than before, and I can't believe my own ears. There is a strange man's voice echoing through this house's thin walls, a voice completely unknown. Clearly, an intruder I don't know is speaking to Nurse Grace in the living room. I can distinguish both of their voices now, the man's softer and calm, the other, Nurse Grace's, insistent and loud.

It appears that she is quite distraught—I have never heard her speak with this level of emotion before. Nurse Grace is clearly disturbed, even angry at what is being said. Who could this stranger be, why is he upsetting her so thoroughly, and what might he possibly be saying that would cause her such alarm? Although I am not able to decipher exactly how Nurse Grace is answering his questions, it is not hard to recognize the distress in her voice.

I feel a moment of pure panic.

Something unanticipated is taking place downstairs.

What am I to do? Return to my room and close the door? Lie back in bed and pretend to have never awakened? Close my eyes and hope that the intrusion will soon be over, that a comfortable silence will once again fill all hallways of my house? But the idea of a stranger downstairs right below me, someone evidently unwelcome and causing disturbance, overwhelms me with anxiety. And if Mademoiselle had the wherewithal, she would most certainly be displeased.

I am frozen in place, cornered upstairs, flat against a wall. I hear Nurse Grace's voice raised to another octave; I hear her yelling and then a sudden moment of silence all over again.

Nurse Grace's bedroom door, directly in front of me, suddenly flies open as if someone is trying to escape from inside, and I lose all breath. The door swings back and forth for a moment until I realize that it is propelled by a breeze coming from the interior window, and I find myself following the small ripple of air all the way into Nurse Grace's room. As I reach to pull the window shut, I am horrified at what I see outside. I can hardly believe my eyes.

My worst nightmare has come true.

Parked right in front of the house, below this very bedroom window, is a police car, clear as day. It is painted black, just as in my imagination, and there is a round silver siren and a long yellow and red light on top. I open the window further in order to see more closely. On the side of the car facing the house, in large white letters, the words GENEVA COUNTY POLICE are spelled out. And then, directly under: IN AN EMERGENCY CALL 911.

For a moment I lose all of my faculties. For a minute I consider the emergency at hand and actually think about calling 911.

And then I remember that the problem is the police themselves, that the enemy is within; the man downstairs, in my own house, is probably just doing his job, that of investigating a crime of some sort. It is obvious that he is not here simply to cause trouble, but that he is searching for answers, trying to uncover the truth of some kind. Perhaps he is just canvassing the neighborhood, attempting to assess the composure of the residents in the wake of all the sniper shootings, collect undiscovered evidence and identify possible witnesses for trial. But perhaps he already knows who is guilty, exactly who the criminal is, and has come to confront the culprit, having followed a trail of clear, undeniable clues.

It was bound to happen eventually, anyway. There is no real way to avoid this moment, keep the the truth from being discovered, my secret from being told. I have known this from the beginning and, on some level, anticipated this very day. It is suddenly clear to me that the police have figured out the mystery. The evidence speaks for itself, the eyewitness accounts credible, the man downstairs most definitely an investigator, grilling Nurse Grace with questions about my whereabouts on the days and nights of the sniper shootings, of the horrendous, murderous crimes.

Of course the police know nothing about my life, about the secret of my birth and of my brother. How would anyone of sound mind ever consider the possibility that my twin is still viable, that he is still alive? Even I know that this is a somewhat irrational presumption on my part, and that the probability of his existence is negligible, that there probably isn't anyone out there who looks just like me but who has a heart of different dimensions and a malignant soul.

Still, the shootings aren't figments of my imagination. I haven't made up the horrendous violence spread all over the news. There is concrete evidence of these sniper attacks, cold-hearted murders. And it seems that someone matching my appearance could very well be responsible for these crimes.

Surely, it is I the police will think guilty. It is I who fits the descriptions. I am the one to be apprehended and punished for someone else's sordid crimes. How I wish I could talk to my grandmother, how I wish I could turn to her for advice, the only other one who knows the secret shame of my birth. But I cannot, and I must face this crisis on my own, no longer a boy but now a man.

Clearly, the true culprit is still out there, filled with fury and resentment, possibly the cause of my oncoming demise. Only I know the murders will not end with my capture. A life for me in captivity, locked away in prison, won't solve anything at all, and the deaths of the beloveds will continue; they will have locked up the wrong man.

Shall I escape from my enemy before the inevitable happens, or will I be forced to give up my other, made to speak of what should not ever be known? Should I consider bolting and hiding in the roof's deepest eaves or find refuge in the basement, behind the broken freezer, inside the false cellar wall?

Should I consider running straight out the back door?

But before I can do anything, I hear the front door closing and look out the window again to see the policeman. He is probably a detective of some kind since he is clearly out of uniform, wearing an ordinary brown business suit, heading toward his car. He stops suddenly and looks back at the house for a moment as if mystified, and then shakes his head slowly.

Has he caught a glimpse of my shadow hidden behind the upstairs window? Will he decide to turn around and march back into the house in order to arrest me and place me behind bars?

To my amazement and relief, the man does nothing for a minute. He stands there in front of the house without moving a single muscle, then all at once he opens the car door and slides inside. Then I hear the engine sputter, grow louder, and before I know it, the police car is speeding down the street, around the corner, until I cannot see it anymore.

I quickly shut the window and make my way out of Nurse Grace's bedroom. The woman is to be thanked, I think to myself; it's clear she has defended me against my predator, guarded against the enemy knocking at my door. She has refused to let the detective arrest me and take me to the police station downtown. Nurse Grace is my protector; she has done her best to keep me from harm.

I walk slowly down the stairs and head into the kitchen. I sit down at the table as if nothing has happened, as if there has been no intrusion, no one asking questions or trying to uncover the closely guarded secrets of my past.

As usual, Nurse Grace is preparing breakfast with a vengeance. She is bent over the counter, immersed in stirring furiously, trying to pulverize a thick batter in a large green glass bowl. When she turns to look at me, she smiles weakly, and wipes her eyes with the back of one hand.

Is it my imagination or has Nurse Grace been crying? Her eyes are red, her face is mottled, she avoids my glance with the lowering of her lids. What, exactly, did the detective say to cause her such distress, and does she, despite herself, doubt the boy sitting before her in the kitchen chair? Am I to blame for Nurse Grace's unhappiness—has she put herself in jeopardy while keeping me from harm?

I hang my head and try to ignore these unpleasant thoughts. There's one thing for certain, one fact undoubtedly true: This woman preparing my breakfast is my advocate, my guardian, someone to be appreciated and admired. I must not take Nurse Grace for granted anymore, in fact I will do my best to get along with her and make her as comfortable as possible while staying with me in this house.

I watch as she pours maple syrup over a stack of blueberry pancakes. I see her hands shake as she drops a large marshmallow in a steaming mug of hot chocolate. I want desperately to ask her a question, find out exactly what happened, what the detective asked her and how she replied, but I remain silent.

I find myself wishing for her to stop what she is doing for a moment and sit down right by my side.

But Nurse Grace seems intent on finishing the preparation of my breakfast and passes me a small bowl of fruit salad. "Just as an appetizer before your pancakes," she says softly. "I'm keeping the main course warm until you're ready for it. There's nothing worse than a stack of flapjacks gone cold."

What was that she once called this fruit salad—"Ambrosia, the food of the gods."

I dig my spoon into the box of confectioners' sugar by her elbow. I will sprinkle the ambrosia until it is glazed with glistening powder. I will have a mound of sweet fruit and syrupy pancakes for my breakfast.

I will please my caretaker, my provider, my sentry, this unexpected friend.

Comprehensive supportive treatment is necessary for survival and future health.

I will fill my stomach completely.
I will eat until nothing is left anymore.

· DAY EIGHT ·

GRACE

Yet another shooting is reported in this morning's paper, and Grace can hardly believe her eyes.

This last victim is a bus driver, an ordinary citizen, apparently a decent guy, minding his own business and trying to support his family the very best way he knew how. What a shame, what a tragedy that a life like this can end all of a sudden without warning. Grace finds herself wondering if this man leaves behind a family, a wife, children, a lover. How they must be suffering.

Murdered out of thin air. Completely random and unpredictable.

This is what Grace finds terrifying. How one's world can be turned inside out at a moment's notice. Again, no trace of the shooter. No evidence found. Not a single bullet shell or another tarot card. Nothing at all.

Grace shudders and turns the paper over. She won't read any more of this horrifying news for now, nor will she speak of today's murder to the boy. He's been exposed to enough. No, Grace won't discuss this last crime with Noah this morning over breakfast, as she has done the days before. Instead she'll bake a ham and cheese omelet and have it ready, all puffed up beautifully golden and warm, before Noah even wakes up. Or maybe pancakes—a thick stack coated with butter and syrup. But just as she prepares to crack the eggs into a glass bowl, there's a knocking at the front door. Grace looks at her watch: 8:15 A.M.—who could possibly be visiting at such an early hour on a weekday morning?

For a moment, she's afraid. The knocking stops for a minute, and then begins again.

Grace feels oddly unnerved, unable to decide what to do. Should she respond to the relentless rapping, should she open the door and make herself vulnerable to who knows what? After all, the very face of evil may be lurking right outside: there's so much senseless violence prowling the streets at every turn.

The knocking continues and Grace worries that the persistent noise will be heard upstairs. She wipes her hands on her apron, slowly heads to the front hall, approaches the door tentatively, then presses her ear to its center, as if this will somehow help her to identify what waits on the other side.

More knocking. She jumps.

"Who's there?" Grace hears her voice, shaky and hollow at first, then louder and yet louder again. "Who's there? Please identify yourself."

"Geneva County Police, ma'am. Detective Brian Hinkle. We spoke on the phone. Do you mind if I come in?"

Grace steps back from the door and suddenly doesn't know what to do. She feels terror creep up her back until her entire spine aches.

What does this man, this ignorant detective, want with her, and what on earth is he doing outside a lonely boy's small house? How did he even find her, anyway? She can't remember giving him an address.

Grace has no intention of opening the door and letting Detective Hinkle inside, but she can't quite figure out how to turn him away. And any disturbance is the last thing in the world that this household needs.

"Miss Rush? Sorry to bother you so early in the morning. Do you mind if I come in and talk to you for a moment? I'll just take a few minutes of your time."

What should she do? She sighs and rubs her hands together until she can practically see her own flesh steam. And then, before she knows it—in fact, she hardly realizes what she is doing at all—she slides off the chain lock and turns the latch.

A tall middle-aged man stands there awkwardly for a moment, carrying a tattered, stained brown leather briefcase in one hand. A ream of torn yellow paper pokes up from an exposed pocket. The briefcase clearly can barely hold its contents, papers crammed in haphazardly and spilling over the sides. One floats to the ground but the detective doesn't seem to notice. He's staring at her expectantly.

"Miss Rush?"

She nods.

"Detective Hinkle. We spoke on the phone the other day."

Why does the man repeat himself? She knows who he is. She knows that they spoke on the phone. She isn't an idiot.

"May I come in?"

He flashes a silver badge.

She nods again, but doesn't move.

He walks around her until he's all the way inside. Grace still doesn't move. She hears him take a deep breath.

Finally, she closes the door slowly and then turns to study the stranger standing in front of her. He has a surprisingly large profile, with the stooped posture of the very tall, and a round, flushed face. He's perspiring, and tiny beads of sweat glisten on his forehead, dampening the tips of his bangs.

She's reminded of a child after swimming. He looks more like an overgrown boy than a man. His sandy hair, wispy at the temples and wavy on top, hangs uncombed over his ears.

The man clearly needs a haircut. And a fresh shirt as well. The collar is frayed, the white fabric soiled, and the top button just above the knot of his tie is missing.

"I know it's early. Sorry to bother you this time of morning."

Does he have to continue repeating the same damn thing again and again? And if he's so intent on being a pain in the neck, why, he can turn right around and leave. He certainly wasn't invited, for god's sake.

Grace narrows her eyes and taps her foot on the floor. She won't ask him to sit down.

"Miss Rush, I know that this is a sensitive topic. I know that you didn't want to discuss it over the phone. But since I was in the general area on other police business—you know, this last shooting was just a bit down the road—well, I thought I could stop by in person for a moment and give you something that I think you might want. I hope you don't mind the intrusion without any warning, but as I'm working the area . . ." His voice trails off for a moment and then continues. "Anyway, I checked with the powers that be and got approval to give you this address."

The detective's eyes are pale blue, surrounded by folds of sunburned skin. Grace judges him to be in his early forties, or maybe even a bit younger than that. And his forehead is furrowed with surprisingly deep creases, as if he is in deep thought, trying to unravel a complicated puzzle. But when he looks down at her, as he does just now, his smile is broad, his expression kind. Perhaps others would consider him decent-looking, maybe even handsome.

"I got to thinking," he continues, bending over to open the briefcase at his side, "with all these shootings, with all the recent tragedies in our town, well, it just seemed to me that we all need to stick together and help each other out now, during this difficult time. And since we were disconnected during our last conversation on the phone, I thought I'd just drop this off to you in person."

Grace wonders how she can stop this man from saying anything more. He doesn't have a right to come here to this house and look right into her tired face. She wants to turn and hide her head; she wants to run; she wants to completely disappear.

There are many things too terrible to acknowledge. Some should remain unspoken for all time. How can this detective, this man she doesn't even know, think he can talk to her about the most personal subject of her entire life?

She will not say a word.

But then, despite herself, for a moment, Grace wants to speak, even just to tell the rude intruder to leave the house, but her tongue is suddenly thick with fury. Why doesn't her mouth move?

She remembers the Scrabble game in the next room and thinks how funny it would be if she spelled out a few choice words for this unwelcome man.

SHUT UP, she would write, the letters arranged just so.

IDIOT

STOP

LEAVE

GO

and worse.

She would spread the wooden squares on the floor right in front of him. She would point down to make her wishes clear.

He would not cross this line of words. He wouldn't dare.

But, for now, Grace can't seem to budge. Her legs are paralyzed. Even her neck is frozen and she is unable to move her head from side to side. If only she could turn her heavy, heavy body, she'd be certain to whip herself around and fly right out of the room.

He would be left standing there, flabbergasted. He wouldn't know what to do.

The detective clears his throat and then slowly offers Grace something retrieved from his briefcase. He extends his large hand and she watches it hang, as if floating unattached, in space.

Don't, please don't.

Grace recoils. She wants nothing from him, nothing at all, but here it is anyway, and there seems nothing she can do but accept the small piece of paper handed to her. She looks down. She's holding a yellow slip of paper, a name and address scrawled on it with large, broad strokes. When she glances up at him, he grins sheepishly, a child waiting to be praised for a job well done.

She doesn't have a thing to say.

How could this man, this pathetic detective, know what she wants at all? Somehow the paper has found its way into her shaking hands, its words growing larger and larger by the minute.

Is she crying, or was the paper already damp?

Grace's hands are trembling. For a moment she thinks she'll fall down.

"Mrs. Rush, Miss Rush, Grace, are you all right? Can I get you anything? A glass of water? Do you want to sit for a while?"

Grace hears the detective's voice booming from somewhere far off, but she shakes her head no.

She inhales deeply and turns the paper over.

She wipes her face with her sleeve and coughs.

She will get through this.

Noah needs her.

She will be strong for him.

Upstairs is another child.

She hands the paper back to Detective Hinkle, but the damage is done: the family's name is burned into her hands.

"No. Please." He shakes his head, refusing, and looks confused. "No, you keep it. I brought it for you, to follow up on when you like. I think the child, the recipient, is a little girl."

His tie is stained with something yellow, perhaps mustard. It's knotted loosely under his collar, and hangs around a thick, sunburned neck. She takes one step toward him and then one back again. Grace wishes nothing more than to smack this detective's insolent, wide, beaming face. She wants to knock him so hard that he will fall to the ground. She desperately wants Detective Hinkle laid out on the floor.

"What makes you think I'm interested in keeping this?" She hears her own voice, loud and strident, the paper clutched, crumpled in her hand. "I want nothing to do with you and nothing to do with this address. I never want to see you around this house. Please, just go away and don't ever come back here or telephone me again."

How surprised he looks, his entire face collapsing, his mouth opening, closing, then opening. The man suddenly looks old.

She feels no sympathy in her hardened pit of a heart.

"What are you waiting for, Detective? Please leave. I don't want to have to ask you again."

Then she takes the crumpled paper, which has stubbornly unfolded again in her cold hand, and tosses it at the metal wastebasket by the front door.

Stunned, he stumbles backward. Did he really think she would be grateful? Did he really think she'd be pleased?

He reaches for his briefcase and shakes his head. Grace notices a blue vein throbbing at his temple. She thinks he'll never leave.

Thank goodness, at least, the man is silent. Thank goodness, he doesn't dare say a word.

But he does leave, after all. He straightens himself up to his full height, rubs his head with one hand, and then sighs. Grace knows she should say something to him now, something ordinary and well-mannered. "Thank you for your trouble" or "Please let me see you to the door." But she isn't interested in being polite, she isn't even interested in even appearing sane. All she can think about in this moment is getting the detective to leave the house and get out of her sight.

Thank goodness, he does just that.

Thank goodness, she's left alone.

• • •

That night, Grace dreams of a childhood vacation at the beach. Her mother sits by her side, beautiful, as she was so many years ago, her hair inky black and clipped in a short bob, and the two of them, parent and child, are digging together in the warm sand. The tide slides forward, but Grace continues to shovel pure white grains into a blue plastic bucket, while her mother stretches out her long tanned legs all the way to the water's edge.

The sea foam looks edible, delicious, fluffy as the cotton candy from the long boardwalk just beyond, and Grace reaches out to scoop a soft mound into her cupped hand, but just as she leans over, a child, a small girl, no, a boy, appears. Wait. It's both.

Twin heads, one male, one female, with a single body emerge from the surf like some kind of sea creature, both monster and mermaid. First, the enormous, bloated heads of the deformed, then the lovely, lithe body of a young child, skin glittering with heart-shaped silver scales. But before Grace can reach out, the children disappear again, and there is nothing left behind except a wet imprint in the sand.

"Gracie!"

Grace awakens suddenly and bolts upright in bed. Has someone been calling out to her, or does this pitiful little voice belong to the long night, of her incomplete dream?

She turns on the light next to her bed and listens.

Nothing.

Grace shivers. She could swear someone called out; the voice was clear as day. Maybe she's going crazy, finally losing her mind? Well, there's certainly no going back to sleep now that she's woken up; she might as well get up and heat up some warm milk to drink downstairs. She looks at the foot of her bed for her bathrobe and shivers. Why is this infernal house always freezing, how is it possible for a home to be this cold? And smack in the middle of summer?

Grace looks out the window, but can barely see a thing. The rough shapes of trees flicker, but the rest of the landscape outside is still black. She stands, stretches, and looks at the time: two A.M.

She'll never be able to go back to sleep. Too much on her mind.

She regrets having blown up at the detective. She's embarrassed not to have remained in control. After all, he was just trying to help, and the accident and its aftermath weren't his fault. Even though it still makes her feel ill, it was sort of considerate of him to make the trip. She supposes that it was thoughtful to even care.

She wraps the belt around her waist tightly. The folds of the soft fabric bunch up and she wraps it again more securely. Is it her imagination or does the long garment hang on her loosely? Is the belt itself too long, too large?

With all the recent distractions, and her devotion to preparing healthy meals, could it be that Grace herself has benefited? Could it be that, through her focus on someone else's need, all of her recent attention on the boy, she's dropped a few pounds this past week, lost some of the excess weight carried for so long?

The irony of the past seven days suddenly occurs to her; she thinks of Noah and smiles. One shrinks while the other broadens, one becomes smaller while the other expands. She knots her belt tightly and opens her bedroom door. There's a fresh quart of milk in the refrigerator downstairs, and half a watermelon carefully scooped into small balls. She'll sit at the table for a while, slowly sipping the comforting drink, and maybe even nibble on a bowl of fruit even though it's the middle of the night. She'll try not to think about the faceless murderer, combing the streets day and night, an enormous rifle carried like a child against his chest. She'll try not to imagine the car as it screeched to a halt against her brother's tiny body and then sped away. She'll try not to be afraid.

Since the kitchen seems to be the warmest, most comfortable room in the entire house, Grace decides to sit there for a good while, despite the late hour, attempting to relax, putting all thoughts of evil out of her mind, enjoying the quiet and thinking over the events of the long, difficult day.

Perhaps it's time to start to accepting what's happened, what's been lost and what's been left behind. Maybe she'll even root through the foyer's small copper wastebasket in search of something recently thrown away.

· DAY NINE ·

NOAH

I will not read the news this morning. In fact, I will not be here when the paper is delivered again.

My decision to leave this house is not an easy one to make, but I arrive at it by dawn, after a troubled night's sleep. Lying in bed awake for most of the night, my deliberance interrupted with short bouts of drowsing and dream, I come to my resolution slowly, fitfully, with anguish and pain.

It finally seems, however, that my options are limited after yesterday's alarming visitor and his confrontation with Nurse Grace. Now that outsiders have arrived and the police have made their presence known and put me on notice, my hand has been forced, whether anyone realizes it or not. There is no doubt that the very worst has happened, that my most dreaded fear of being found out, my secrets revealed for all the world to see, has come to pass; I am left with only one choice, as unfortunate as that choice may be.

Nurse Grace's protection will go only so far. No matter how devoted, she may not be able to prevail.

I am acutely aware that this is probably the worst possible time to disappear. There are important things to take care of during the next few days, obligations to be met, my grandmother to think of. But I am left without a choice.

If I remain here in this house, all will be made public, and they will question me under a spotlight, making me confess every sin. Or they will cuff and imprison me, convinced that my brother's revenge is my own.

I am cornered, back to the wall, and there simply seems no possible way out. It won't be long before the uniformed officers arrive, swarming my front lawn, sirens blasting, guns drawn, possibly even waving an enormous bull-horn outside in the thin air.

How the neighbors will stare, how they will rush to call one another on the telephone. Yes, we always knew he was an odd boy, a very strange young man, no wonder our children avoided him, no wonder he has no friends. It simply isn't normal for a youngster to spend all day inside a darkened house with an invalid grandmother. We knew something peculiar was afoot, we always were convinced, but for goodness' sake, what could we have done? Thank the Lord that our own children are different, that they are normal, our family well balanced, no bad blood in our history. Thank goodness we have escaped such horror, mortification, disturbed behavior of any kind and are able to walk the circumference of ordinary family life without stumbling or missing a single step.

Thank goodness he isn't our child, that this isn't our house.

But don't they know that all can be changed without warning? Don't they realize that, any minute, something unforeseen might occur? How summer lightning will strike for no reason, obliterating the landscape—how even an entire family can disappear from view? They think their days are lived safely, their children protected from harm, but I unfortunately know otherwise. I understand how a whole life can be split in half, divided, how a heart can be carved unmercifully without warning, how insufficient blood can result in unmitigated, permanent injury.

They may hide behind their window curtains. They may cluck their tongues and cross their arms in disgust. And still, I wish them nothing less than pure happiness. I do not wish others anything but the best.

And then there is the question of Nurse Grace. Of course, she would be unable to escape the scandal, the rumors, the fervor surrounding my escape. Every time she ventured outside in the morning to pick up the newspaper, or go shopping, there would be unavoidable whispers and there would be constant stares. No one watching would dare say anything to her face but would hide themselves behind half-closed doors, and my unfortunate nurse would be forced to answer the police's probing, insensitive questions about me and provide them access to all corners of the house.

Maybe there would even be unnecessary force used in an effort to coerce her into talking, in making her allow them upstairs without an official warrant, without following the proper procedures for such an inappropriate, voracious search. Maybe they will rummage furiously through the entire dwelling, even disturb the quiet of my poor grandmother's dim room.

"Over here!" a sergeant will call. "I found something. Look in this closet. More evidence, a scrapbook, a journal. Come see right here."

They will dust for fingerprints. They will take samples of minuscule fibers from the carpet, from the bed linens, from all clothes. They will clear off my shelves in a single sweep, they will look for clues with unblinking eyes. They will touch my beautiful books, one by one.

No, better that I not be here when they come for me. Better that I disappear without a word. I rub my eyes and stretch. As usual, the air is frigid and I am cold. I rise, neatly stack the books spread on the floor, and prepare to make my bed. My army corners are impeccable, just as

Mademoiselle taught me: the sheets smooth, the pillowcase unwrinkled as if it had never supported a human head. There is a small satchel in the back of the closet, the very one that contained my little clothes when I first moved here so many years ago, and it has the mixed odor of talcum and mold, the lingering fragrance of both the very young and the dead.

I carefully button three blue cotton shirts, fold them neatly into squares, then the same for three pairs of khaki trousers, some underwear, and my favorite soft gray socks. Two thin books will fit nicely into the case's outside compartment, and it is simply too difficult to choose, so I turn my head and blindly select the volumes. I pack them without opening my eyes.

Money is the next issue to be addressed, and fortunately I have saved my birthday gifts from Mademoiselle, year after year. Each anniversary spent with her in this house was rewarded with a personal check for ten dollars, always delivered to me through the mail, although my grandmother was right upstairs.

"Not to spend on yourself," she would

chide. "Children don't need indulgences, not to waste on silly toys. Save this money for something substantial, my dear. Put it away, and you may need it for an important purchase one day, perhaps even for an emergency. You never know when disaster will strike, darling. I guess you already know about that."

Funny how I never considered disobeying her by spending my birthday money on books or some childish whim. She never would have known. She probably never would have really even cared.

Strange how I bowed to her wishes all that time, never having the opportunity to recognize my own.

For years, the minute I awoke on my birthday morning, I would rush to see if the mail had arrived, if that particular letter could be found. And every year, without fail, there it would be, the same perfumed, pink floral envelope inscribed with Mademoiselle's shaky scrawl. But when I eagerly tore it open, desperate to see what was inside, I would always be disappointed, defeated by the familiar contents. Year after year, it was the same slip of paper that drifted to the floor, the same check for ten dollars made out in my name. But, no matter how much I hoped, no matter how much I wished, there would never be a birthday card or a personal note of any kind.

Why, I think to myself now, why did I expect anything different year after year? Why did I not learn my lesson once and for all, and stop pathetically hoping for more? Other children received best wishes, I was certain of that. Other children were indulged on their birthdays. What had I done not to deserve the same?

As if my birth were an embarrassment. As if that day were to be ignored.

I open my top dresser drawer slowly and count the one-dollar bills inside. Luckily, Mademoiselle had taken me to cash the checks each year at the bank or I would have nothing but a collection of paper. The annual pilgrimage was a firm tradition, but it wasn't until now that I really appreciate the gift.

When she was younger, before she took to her bed, my grandmother would spend my birthday morning preparing for our yearly cashing of my check, sitting in front of her dressing table for what seemed like hours, styling her brittle black hair, then violently spraying it all over so that both of our eyes would tear. And then there was the application of makeup, the meticulous process of applying crumbling powder several times until it was perfectly set. After, there would always be a dusting of violet eyeshadow left on her sunken cheeks, casting her complexion off-color, making her look somewhat nauseated and ill.

And then she would turn to her closet, wrestling with the agonizing decision of what in the world to wear. She would hold each plastic-covered dress disdainfully, the sharp hangers dangling, sigh and mournfully shake her head. Every dry cleaner's bag contained a different outfit, visible through the wrapping, yet still difficult to see. She would drop them, one by one, to the floor, exasperated, and the plastic would puff up with air, making the clothing seem gigantic, even though there was only a tiny slip of a dress within. But eventually Mademoiselle would resolve herself to the challenge of finding the perfect choice for that particular day. It felt like forever as she tried on different selections, desperately searching for the exact one.

"Does this suit my coloring, darling?" she would ask as I sat upright on her beige velvet chaise. "Is the skirt too short? Do you think my legs pretty? Is this dress too tight, cut too low, too old-fashioned, too ordinary, does it make me look too fat, too grandmotherly, too old?"

Thank goodness I knew enough to say nothing. I would sit there silently and simply smile. I used to think my grandmother quite beautiful in a dramatic, frightening kind of way. I used to think that she looked like a glamorous film star.

I had seen old horror movies with Joan Crawford. I had watched Bette Davis and Olivia de Havilland. They all shared the same dark lipstick, shaven eyebrows, heavy lids, eyes that drooped at the corners, shellacked, immobile hair.

Then, a few minutes before three o'clock, just as the bank was to close, Mademoiselle would instruct me to find her car keys and examine my appearance from head to toe. No loose threads were acceptable, no stains, no scuffed shoes, no stray hairs out of place.

Once satisfied, we would leave together, making sure the house was locked up tight and that there were no lights left on inside. And then we would slowly roll to the bank, headlights glowing, as if in a funeral procession, seated upright in her huge black Buick, a car large enough to accommodate an entire family of four. But it would be just the two of us, a grandmother and her nervous grandchild, Mademoiselle spinning the steering wheel with one hand and studying her reflection in the narrow mirror above. Sometimes she would whip out a silver lash curler from her purse and clamp it decisively over one eye. She then would have the appearance of an aged, hunched pirate, metallic patch gleaming, her vision impaired, although she was still determined to navigate, to drive dead ahead.

The bank was only six blocks away, and my grandmother always parked at the meter across the street, but absolutely refused to ever pay. When we returned from our errand, there was usually a ticket, one that would immediately be thrown away.

She did not believe in paying good money as a patron of town businesses. She thought they should accommodate her needs instead.

But first we would enter the bank together, my following behind her in tentative baby steps, Mademoiselle holding her head up like royalty, shoulders thrown back, her gait confident and determined, her posture perfectly erect. She would greet everyone who passed with a hand-shake, even those I am certain she didn't know, and then clear a path, no matter how crowded the room, how long the lines. She would demand her money from the teller with a flourish and then offer me the bills with a leather-gloved hand.

I look down at the cash I am holding. Ten dollars times ten years. One hundred dollars minus the fifteen for my impulsive purchase of the Scrabble game last year: eighty-five dollars. That should get me pretty far. I roll the money into a thick wad and slip it in my pocket. I feel suddenly powerful, grown up, proud.

The early morning light is dappled, making

the outside world appear artificial, like a colorless painting, a faded photograph, a pale universe imagined from the grave. I pull the blinds
and check to see that all windows are locked,
that no one can enter or exit without being
heard.

And then, as if there is nothing at all
unusual, I creep quietly down the stairs, through
the hallway, and toward the front door. It is just
past dawn, and as always, the entire house is
silent, each room before me filled with a ghostly
early morning haze. I imagine Mademoiselle's
door to be tightly shut, without a crack left open
to accommodate either light or air.

The thought of my grandmother greatly dis-
tresses me; I know that this is the wrong time to
leave, and that I am not behaving properly, as
taught. After all, she was the only one who took
me in when I was helpless and completely alone.
Where would I be if not for her? Where would I
live? In some kind of institution, some derelict,
orphan children's home?

But remaining here is clearly not the answer.
I am of no use to anyone right now; in fact, it is

possible that if I stay, I could actually do harm.

I pass the kitchen and glance inside. There is a half-filled glass of milk on the table, along with a bowl of watermelon cubes. It's clear that Nurse Grace has been at it again, perhaps indulging in an evening snack without bothering to clean up after herself. I pour the milk in the sink and rinse out the glass. I cover the watermelon with tinfoil and place it in the refrigerator to chill.

Nurse Grace's large plaid flannel bathrobe is draped over the back of a chair and I fold it neatly into a soft mound. The fabric is frayed, worn, as if very old, and it emanates a fragrance reminiscent of the woman it adorns. I hold the folded robe to my nose for a minute and close my eyes. What is this scent that comforts me so?

Citrus and maple syrup, chocolate and honey, nutmeg and clove.

Leaving is more difficult than I anticipate. This small house, now filled with traces of her presence, has suddenly become home. Strange how so much can be altered in just a single week.

But duty calls, and I know what must be done. I slip my battered satchel over my shoulder and straighten my back. Shall I pack some food from the kitchen, or will I make too much noise to safely escape? Maybe a few graham crackers, since the box is left out on the kitchen counter. Maybe an orange, a banana from the bowl on the table, and some biscuits in the bread box baked fresh by Nurse Grace each and every day. An empty jug filled with tap water. A small jar of peanut butter. Some strawberry jam—thank goodness it all fits into my case. Who knows where I will end up in my travels, but for now, the better prepared I am, the more likely I am to persevere, to survive.

The door slams behind me as I leave, and I am startled, anxious not to awaken the sleeping upstairs. But clearly my escape is successful.

No one calls for me, no one follows, no one is even aware that I have gone.

The story of my entire pathetic half life.

But when I am all the way outside, and the fresh air hits me, I all at once recognize my own impulsivity and the sheer lunacy of my foolish plan. Where is a boy to go without direction? How will he find his way without any help?

While I have read about adventures of sailors near the arctic circle and the beauty of Germany and Switzerland, I am coherent enough to understand that I barely have the means to travel out of state, much less to a different country or continent. Perhaps I will begin my journey by visiting the city hospital across town, the very place where I was born, and see if I can acquire funds by becoming the subject of a scientific study, even by selling my own blood. At least this will be a starting point to my new life and a way of supporting myself for a short while before moving on to other things and other places.

The sun is rising before me; it must be close to six o'clock, and the morning light is blinding.

For a minute I cannot see what is in front of me, then notice an object at my feet, something thick yet oblong, an unusual, unfamiliar shape. Maybe a creature the size of a kitten, some kind of animal wound up in sleep. I blink, look closer, and recognize my own error. My vision must be faltering, what I have seen isn't really there at all. There is nothing alive and breathing at my doorstep, not a cat, not a kitten, not a puppy, stray dog, wild rabbit, or baby raccoon. Only the morning newspaper rests there lifeless, rolled up and covered with a black plastic bag, tightly wrapped in a thick shroud from the elements, protection from inevitable summer thunderstorms.

Strange to have thought of something inanimate as breathing, of something inert as alive. Just wishful thinking, I suppose, but it would be pleasant to feel a small heart beating, to gather a warm being under my shirt, close to my chest, nestled soft against my cold, rough skin. It might slip down beneath to my waist. It might shift position, flattening a tender belly over my own, and covering the raised scar on my torso. It might even soothe the wound.

A small, stray beast, another to keep me company during my exile, and to provide comfort during the lonely nights ahead. This, however, is clearly a journey to be taken alone.

And since a companion is hardly the issue, only my imagination playing tricks on my fevered brain, I must address the realistic facts of my departure. Where to go. How to be safe.

How to keep myself hidden from harm.

Perhaps it would be smart to take the newspaper with me. Something else to read. Material to keep me current regarding the murders, as well as abreast of the police's future moves. The rolled paper fits under one arm neatly; I will not even have to adjust my shoulder strap one inch.

I take a step off the cement stoop and then stumble.

I walk forward into nothing at all.

GRACE

The day immediately begins on an odd note.

When Grace opens the front door to look for the newspaper, it's missing from its usual place on the steps, the first time in nine days. Somehow she finds this unsettling, since she's eager to learn about any new developments in the sniper case and unhappy to be left in the dark. For all she knows, there could have been another murder. In fact, there might have been a new shooting right down the street, perhaps even next door. Who knows, with all of this insanity.

Oh, well, maybe it's for the best that there's no paper to read today. Better not to become obsessed with the murders, and certainly healthier to keep more gruesome details away from the boy. He seems so affected by the news of the shootings, seems to take it all to heart, that maybe they both could use a break from the news this morning and concentrate on other, more positive things.

Noah's sleeping late today anyway. It's already eight o'clock, and Grace is used to hearing his footsteps on the stairs by seven. Probably just reading in bed, unless he simply overslept.

No matter. She'll have time to bake the boy his favorite blueberry muffins and poach some rosy Bartlett pears in honey-lemon stock. They're difficult to peel, her thick fingers clumsy, the skin delicate; it's hard not to nick the fruit's fragile flesh. But how lovely when finished, revealed perfectly white. The pears balance upright in a pan of sweet liquid, trembling and exposed, but will remain firm when finally tasted. At least, she hopes they don't soften too much while cooking, that they don't fall apart. The trick is in the timing, not to simmer too long over too intense a flame. The temperature must be perfect, not too hot or cold.

By nine o'clock, she's worried. Maybe Noah's become ill, come down with a fever or a cold, and she should sneak into his room to check. But she hesitates to intervene, knowing that his privacy is important, and decides to wait another hour. By ten, she'll investigate if he still isn't up.

She thinks of Noah and finds herself smiling. How sweet he was last night at dinner, although he didn't say a word. It was as if he sensed her sadness, understood that she was grieving, but how in the world could this young boy know such a thing? Could it be possible? No, Grace thinks, and yet . . .

Somehow she felt the boy's compassion—for the first time, she was aware of his warmth.

It wasn't as if there was anything specific. Just the way he looked at her, the kindness of expression, how he helped to clean the table after they had eaten, how he offered to dry the dishes with a simple wave of a hand. And wasn't she surprised to find him later at the Scrabble table, the board unfolded, the two bags of wooden words in place? She seated herself on the couch right next to him. She was happy to finally be at his side.

It was as if the boy had suddenly, finally, begun to come to life.

Once more, they played the game in silence, but this time they finished without one leaving the other behind.

They sat there for over an hour. At least that.

They didn't bother to keep score.

By ten o'clock she climbs the stairs two by two, as if in a run. Quite amazing, considering the heft of her large body, that she's able to move so quickly when she needs to. As usual his door is shut, and she listens for a moment, ear to the door. But she hears nothing, nothing moving, nothing at all stirring inside.

The door is soundless as it opens, not a creak, not a squeal, and she gasps at the empty room before her. No boy sleeps in his carefully made double bed.

He's not in the closet, not hiding behind the draperies, not in the bathroom, completely vanished from sight. What should she do, where else to look, who should she call, what if he's never to be found?

But there's no reason to panic, is there, at least not for now. Where could a thirteen-year-old boy possibly find to go so early in the morning, before he's even eaten a single thing? He's probably outside walking, a short trip to the store, or on some kind of special errand. Maybe visiting the library or discovering something new to purchase at the local bookshop.

Would anything be open so early in the day? Maybe the town library hours are unusual during the summer, maybe they encourage children to visit first thing, so that they have the rest of the day to play outdoors.

But in her heart of hearts, she knows better. Noah's not one to wander, to roam here and there. In fact, during their nine days together, he's never taken one single step out of the house. She'd assumed it was his grandmother who kept him near, the need he felt to stay as close as possible to her room, to maintain a constant vigil despite the circumstances, and although at first Grace thought it odd that he didn't have a need to venture elsewhere, it never troubled her very much.

Now, however, something is different. The boy is missing, gone, disappeared into thin air. Where could he possibly be, and for how long?

Grace sits down at the kitchen table, her hands trembling, her whole body quaking with a familiar dread. Noah is her responsibility and she has no idea where he is or what to do. Should she wait patiently to see what's to happen, or should she call someone to help her find him right now? Maybe her supervisor should be informed immediately, but Grace is hesitant to sound the bells of alarm. If she reports Noah missing, then who knows what could happen, and where the boy might eventually be sent. Social Services doesn't like it when children run away and will insist on closer monitoring, maybe even placing him in a group home with delinquent, troubled boys.

No, this clearly isn't the answer. There must be another option. Another possibility. Some way to look for Noah without alerting the authorities to his absence, to this recent, unthinkable event.

Grace looks down at her watch and can

hardly believe it. Already 11:30 and no sign of anything. She's tempted to telephone the neighbors, but then realizes she can't remember any of their names. She certainly could appear on their front steps, but these days, no one is opening their doors.

Twelve o'clock and Grace is frantic.

What to do, where to go, who to call?

She finds her address book on the counter and riffles through the pages, looking for who knows what.

Then a name and number suddenly come to her. It's printed clearly in the back. She stares down for a moment and hesitates. Will he be in, will he be willing, can he help? Maybe he won't even answer her call after her impolite behavior when he stopped by the house.

She's surprised when the detective answers, then remembers having the number to his direct line.

His voice is steady, reassuring. He'll be right over. At least as soon as possible, but is she absolutely sure that the boy has disappeared? This kind of thing happens all the time. Boys will be boys. The kid will return before she knows it. He'll find his way back home. Don't worry, everything will work out just fine.

She's embarrassed by his kindness. She didn't expect such a helpful response.

She tells him she's sorry. That she regrets her rudeness during his visit before—it was hardhearted not to accept his kindness, his generous compassion and concern for her pain, for her brother, for own lovely Liam, her beloved, her little boy lost.

She breaks down. She's sobbing.

Not another lost boy.

She'll try to be calm while waiting, but can he hurry, will he be here in time?

What if Noah has been abducted, what if he's being held against his will?

What if the sniper were to find him, targeting the child through his scope?

What if the bullet penetrates deeply, what if there's no antidote?

What if Noah is injured, lying somewhere alone and in pain?

·　　·　　·

When the detective finally arrives, it's a miracle. It's already almost four o'clock. He regrets not making it sooner, but something urgent came up, a crisis that needed tending right then and there. Something related to the sniper case. He'll tell her about it later, when there's time.

She was worried that he had forgotten. She'd sat in a dead panic, not moving from the chair. She thought he wouldn't come at all, that he had changed his mind. After all, she realizes that he has an important job to do, a killer to catch, evidence to gather. Her problem is hardly comparable to that.

Yet, how relieved she is to see him.

How tall he is. How competent he looks. How pleasant, even though she doesn't deserve such concern. She shrinks when remembering their last encounter, and silently promises herself to never be so impossibly out of control again.

He listens intently, leaning forward, elbows on knees, a sprinkling of pale blond stubble on his cheeks and on his chin. His expression confident, intent. He clearly knows what to do.

Thank goodness, someone else to help her,

even someone who is practically a stranger. Thank goodness there's another human being in this cold, godforsaken house, someone to take over, maybe even to trust.

How much she'd like to lean on the detective, as he talks to her. Drop down her heavy head.

Tired and scared. Head on his shoulder, hand in his hand.

But, of course, this is ludicrous. Grace is losing her mind.

How can she be thinking such things, of herself at all, with Noah out there by himself, all alone? And a man she hardly even knows sitting beside her. She watches carefully as he nods and makes notations on a small notepad with a green ink pen.

He must alert his sergeant, but Social Services can wait. It's best for her to stay where she is in case the boy returns or calls. Don't worry too much, he tells her; he has seen this many times before, probably just a troubled runaway kid. But for now, it's important to stay calm.

How, she asks him, how can she stay here and stay calm?

He shakes his head and takes her arm as if to escort her to a dance. You must. Listen to me, listen. We will start a search immediately and before you know it your boy will be home. Try to get some rest—I'll be sure to call you later no matter what.

But rest isn't available to Grace. She's not able to even sit still. She roams the small house restlessly, looking for some kind of clue, and checks Noah's room several times before turning to the grand-mother's door. Perhaps the boy is hiding there, curled up next to the old woman's bed, but when Grace turns on the lights, he's nowhere to be found.

"Don't worry," she whispers into the still-ness. "Don't worry, we'll find him no matter what." And then she immediately feels guilty for letting the old woman down. Grace had been hired to be useful and to help care for Noah, and now, just look at the outcome. Mademoiselle's grandson is gone.

At five o'clock the detective telephones, but the news is still grim. No sign of the kid anywhere, he reports, but we've got time before dark. At eight: still nothing, not a lead or a clue, but he promises that they're still working and will continue late into the night. At eleven she's hopeless, desperate to hear from the police once more. But the detective won't call again until morning and has instructed her to get some sleep if at all possible, and he will swing by, first thing the next day.

Grace lies on her back in the narrow guest-room bed, staring at the ceiling, at the patterns made by shadow, listening intently for the telephone. Perhaps Noah will call, she thinks—why doesn't he phone and let her know? Where will he sleep tonight, and is he warm enough, is he protected from evil, from harm?

She extends her arms straight above and makes shadow shapes with her fists.

He's not exactly a tough, street-smart boy, is he? Isn't he frightened, out there all alone?

She moves her fingers one by one, then again, two by two.

First the shape of a bunny, then a puppy dog, a kitten, and a sharp-snouted raccoon.

Why do these particular animals come to mind now, why does she think of them? How strange to see her clumsy hands make delicate shapes out of shadow—small, frail creatures in the twilight.

When her little brother was anxious, afraid in the dark, Grace would entertain him with these playmates, companions in the night. And then Liam would giggle, his whole face breaking apart. His laughter was more of a chortle, full-bodied, that of an older child, and he found it difficult to stop.

She remembers him almost hysterical, gasping for breath, his face reddened with the effort of pure pleasure, his arms waving in the air.

How children find comfort in the ordinary, in a loved one's hands.

Simply fingers in the shadow.

The movement of small things.

· DAY TEN ·

NOAH

There are voices above me when I awaken the next morning. I hear footsteps on the hardwood floor.

Then silence.

My mouth is full of dust, my eyes smart, my back aches, and I can't remember how I even ended up here at all. What day is it, where am I, am I dreaming or am I actually awake?

Then I remember. I had only meant to stay here for the day, just until evening came, then planned to begin my real journey, leave the house, the neighborhood, the town, the county, the state. But I realized yesterday, as I attempted my initial flight, that it was safer to find a haven within, rather than walk out into the broad daylight. So after I stepped away from the house with nowhere at all to go, I decided to change my plan dramatically and entered my own basement through the exterior hurricane door.

This was not easily accomplished, in fact quite a daunting task, the bolted door covered with dying vines and surprisingly heavy—almost impossible to hold open wide. But I managed to squeeze myself under by prying the entryway ajar with one hand. The interior steps were narrow, the cellar dark, dank inside. I slipped and almost fell several times before making my way all the way to the bottom, to the graveyard of my own house.

Once within, still more obstacles: how would I manage to keep up my nerve? Where to go, where to hide here in order not to be eventually discovered? The cellar could be the first place the police would investigate, once my escape had been determined. For now, however, I might have a window of opportunity, several hours or so until my absence is discovered. And what would Nurse Grace do then? Would she search for me herself, would she report my disappearance to the authorities, would she break down in tears, blame herself?

I deeply regret the pain and distress to be caused and wish that there was another option that was less difficult. But I am resolved.

Once all the way inside down below, I looked anxiously for a hiding place. The cellar floor was damp and muddy, the walls made of stone, the ceiling beamed and extremely low; it was difficult to see at all. I felt my way timidly along the cold walls, fearful of rodents, bats, worms, snakes, of anything that might be lurking in the deep, and then finally came upon wooden eaves, where the basement butts up against the main floor of the upstairs house. One such corner was gated with a splintered wooden covering, an extremely long and narrow triangular door. I pushed it with my shoulder, but it refused to budge. I kicked and watched it creak slowly open, then stepped backward. I barely had the wherewithal to look all the way inside.

After all, I am a boy with limited courage. I am frightened of most anything unusual, unfamiliar, unknown.

Who would have thought I would end up in

the prison of a cold cellar, filthy and wet, full of breeding bacteria and who knows what else.

But when I finally examined the triangular interior of this far-off closeted space, I was encouraged, my fears put to rest just a bit. The oddly shaped haven was completely empty, the perfect size for a boy to squeeze in his thin frame, the perfect place to rest his tired head. And there I slept—exhausted from being awake the previous night—all through most of the afternoon and apparently the night.

I know this because, after awakening, I heard muffled voices above denoting the time of day; then I crawled out from my corner, from the far reaches of the black cellar's interior and looked up to see a ribbon of light surrounding the gap in the closed hurricane door. What time is it exactly, the minute and the hour? I have no idea. But surely it is early morning, and Nurse Grace is up and talking with someone else.

I am desperate to know who her companion is, what they are saying, what their next move will be. Has my absence been noted? Are they searching? Are they desperate to find me?

My back is hurting, my neck sore, and I feel my stomach grumble. How long since I have eaten or had anything at all to drink? I must keep up my strength by providing for my own nourishment. I take the satchel, but its zipper is stuck, and for a moment I panic. What if I am trapped down here beneath the ground for days with nowhere else to go? What if I pass out from starvation? What if there is nothing left of me anymore?

What if they never find me, if I am lost forever, by myself, eternally alone? Who will even miss me? Maybe Nurse Grace, but only for a short while. In no time, she will have another family to care for, another child, and her memory of me will fade quickly. She will probably not even remember my name.

But soon my worst fears are alleviated and the zipper opens with a final nudge. I gobble two biscuits immediately, without stopping to spread them with peanut butter or jam. Three sips of the tap water, but then I know to wait. I must be careful to preserve my rations. I will not be greedy.

I will monitor my own hunger so that my needs do not become uncontrollable, impossible to be met.

My requirement for food and water addressed, I now discover another pressing concern. My bladder is full and I don't know how much longer I can wait to relieve myself. My eyes have adjusted to the darkness and I look for an opening in the floor, some kind of crack to the outside, perhaps even a hole. I notice the floor of the cellar dips toward the center and find there, in the middle, an indentation, something I quickly assess to be a drain. This is hardly what I am accustomed to, hardly a possibility a well-brought-up boy would consider, but there certainly are no other choices, so I quickly make do with what I determine to be the only way.

If only Mademoiselle could see me now. What on earth would my grandmother have to say?

Now what to do, since my bodily functions have been met—it is clearly much too early to depart the cellar—that must wait until later. At evening, under darkness, I will take my leave, with a specific plan of where to go, how to get there, while maintaining invisibility, anonymity.

For the moment, however, I must find a dry spot under the large hurricane doorway, and try to use the small bits of light for reading one of my books. And then I suddenly remember the newspaper plucked from my doorstep the day before. I find it stuck in the corner of my sleeping closet, and slip off its plastic covering—perhaps something useful for another day. Who knows, perhaps as a makeshift hat to repel dripping water, protection from the elements above, or as an extra bag in which to store provisions or clothes, as my satchel is stuffed to the brim. I compress the wrapping into a small ball and stuff it into the outside compartment of my overflowing case.

The newspaper unrolls as if powered by electricity, then lies flat, awaiting my approach. Not surprising, the ink has been smeared by the damp weather and the print is somewhat difficult to decipher. Still, I am able to manage, despite the blurred words and paltry lighting, and am terrified by what I read. Apparently, there have been no more shootings, but the police are on the verge of an arrest.

A suspect has been identified, although his name and face will not be released to the press at this time. He has yet to be apprehended, but it is reported that they are very close.

It is apparent that I have made the right decision to vanish—it was clearly necessary to have made my escape. As imagined, the police are on their way to find me, the cold trail has warmed, they have uncovered evidence, it all will make sense. So, for now, I will stay hidden in this black coffin, cold and wet, left to decompose underground. If only I can make it through this one single day, if only another night will come quickly, so that I can begin my true leaving, my adventure yet to be known.

Outside, the air is fresher, my path will be clearer: There will be light and there will be sound.

But for now, I will try to make myself comfortable and read the newspaper through and through. Perhaps I will come across more information about my pursuers, where they are headed and how they are approaching the search. But as I scan the words quickly, I am drawn to an outlined paragraph of information, words printed in bold letters, clear, easy to see.

TIPS FOR STAYING SAFE

Police yesterday offered these tips for protection against sniper-style shootings:

· While outside, try to keep moving. A moving target is more difficult to hit than one that is standing still.

· If you must remain in one place in an area where you feel vulnerable, select the darkest part.

· When moving outside, walk briskly in a zigzag pattern.

· If you must stand outside, try to keep some type of protective cover between yourself and any open areas where a sniper might be located.

· If you are fired on in an open area, drop to the ground and roll away. Look for the closest protective cover and run toward it in short, zigzag dashes.

· Remember that a sniper with the right equipment can shoot accurately from about five hundred yards away.

．　．　．

I put the paper down with a deep sigh. I try to imagine the world above me, hordes of terror-ized victims frantically racing through the streets in complete disarray, running for cover without order, zigzagging their way to work, to school, to the store. They dash back and forth, hearts beat-ing wildly, human moving targets, vulnerable to a sniper yards and yards away. Then I briefly try to amuse myself by imagining Nurse Grace in this situation, her wide skirt flying above her in the air, but the image is somehow not funny, only saddens me more and more. What she must think of me—how ungrateful, what a selfish, coldhearted boy.

My heart hurts to think of her disappoint-ment, her confusion, her loss of respect for the child she thought she knew.

After all, it was Nurse Grace who began to make me feel comforted, who refused to let me sleepwalk woodenly, who saw a real human boy.

But the newspaper article remains com-pelling, and I wonder if my instincts are correct: I have no intention of continuing to lead the life of a terrified fugitive, dashing back and forth this way and that, on the alert for protection, for cover, on the constant lookout for harm. No, perhaps it is better to remain here in the deep cellar. After all, the newspaper practically recommends just this.

Select the darkest part of the area, it is written.

Try to keep protective cover between yourself and any open areas where a sniper might be located.

Clearly I have followed these directions perfectly.

A shooter is hardly likely to be located among these deep stone cellar walls.

And yet, it occurs to me with alarm that the article also describes something oddly applicable to my own life, descriptive of the past years lived upstairs. Haven't I always maintained a constant vigil? Have I not survived in a nonsensical, zigzag pattern, swerving around detours, jumping back from hurdles, trying to avoid all obstacles in my path?

Still, even so, even with these manipulations,

my silence, my isolation, my efforts to disappear, there was no way to avoid becoming a target after all.

No matter how I darted and how I dodged, I still endured internal wounds every day of my life. What an incredibly stupid and cowardly way for a boy to live.

It had been Nurse Grace who began to change this lunacy with her enormity, her largesse, her determination to unearth a buried, lost boy. She guarded me like a palace sentry, trying to keep me safe from danger, from unnecessary hurt.

When they came for me, she protected my privacy. She did not give in, even when challenged to the utmost. Even at her own expense.

When I leave here, I think sleepily, resting my back against a cold wall, I will no longer be frightened and invisible, hidden underground. I will build muscle, increase my bulk; I will speak loudly, I will be heard. One day, far in the future, I will thank Nurse Grace for her devotion, and make her proud of the man I have become.

For now, however, maybe a short interval of napping. I will close my eyes and sleep for a while, then resume eating. I will prepare a sandwich of biscuit and peanut butter. I will eat half a banana.

I will be full.

I hear a sudden, high-pitched chattering, a squeaking of some kind, then something brushes over the surface of my hand.

I jump, but it is just a little cricket. Even I am not frightened of that.

The insect disappears as quickly as it arrived, and I listen for its song, but the cellar is soundless, the quiet numbing. My eyelids are heavy, my throat parched, but still I will not drink. Just sleep for a little bit, I tell myself cautiously, wait for a while before reaching for the small jug. If I am to be here for the duration, then water will be essential to survive. Without it, I will become weak and weaker. I will certainly become sick.

Exhausted, I rest my head against the wall. A short nap will do me good, is much needed. I must keep up my strength and fortify my will.

But the dark room around me is suddenly spinning, and the floor beneath slips out of place.

I am staring at the outline of a shadow. It creeps along the stone walls although I sit perfectly still.

Who is here beside me? Who enters this cave?

Have I fallen into a troubled slumber? Am I dreaming, and if so, how will I be able to know?

What if my brother has come to find me? What if he has managed to slip through that heavy door? What if he learned of my disappearance? What if he came to avenge his abandonment, my betrayal of his life? What if he aimed his rifle right at me? What if he shot me in the heart?

How long would I live then, down below, and how could I possibly survive the night without infection setting in?

Would he stay by me as I declined or would he flee?

Would he forgive me at my deathbed?

Would he have a change of heart?

What if my brother has come to comfort me, to forgive all my sins? What if he came to rescue me from harm and not avenge his birth after all, but accept us as two instead of one?

What if we had lived our lives together from the beginning, no surgery, no sacrifice, no separation, never apart? Just the two of us bound forever, with equal strength, with equal opportunity for life.

What if the attachment had been permanent?

What if our love knew no bounds?

What then?

If he had been with me from the beginning, my brother, if there had always been two instead of just one, we would wake up in the morning together, we would eat our breakfast until it was finished. We would share each and every morsel.

We would never be hungry again.

If he were here with me, we would look practically identical, except that his hair would be softer, longer, lighter. It would reflect the sun.

If he were here, I would be awed by his expression: surprise, bewilderment, wonderment, pure joy. His face would be infused with color, his eyes greener than mine, his lips redder, his teeth glistening whiter—each and every single one of them even—his smile wider, his heart larger, his spine like a strong ladder, its stairs solid rungs of unbreakable bone.

We would read out loud to each other often, sitting outside on the grass. Whole pages would be memorized, words tossed off carelessly from both our tongues. We would rush back inside when we were finished, eager for a cold drink and warm food. And there would be an elaborate meal laid out to greet us, glistening with color and rich with flavor. We would eat until we were full.

Late afternoons, we would walk to the library together, the heat of the day dampening our brows and making us sweat. We would laugh, pointing at each other, amused by the other's countenance, by our gleeful expressions, by our sunburns turning bright red.

The library would be cool and welcoming, the stacks dark, mysterious, filled with the adventure of what is yet to be known. We would finger each page carefully, inhaling the fragrance of print and leather, of dusty bindings, comforted by shelves inhabited by old friends.

If he were here with me, we would end our days sipping water from the torn garden hose outside the back door. We would spray each other's clothing until we were both soaking, and then wear our wet sneakers inside, leaving footprints that turned the carpet from blank to burnished. This would delight us both to no end.

Winters, he would shine my jacket buttons with his shirt cuff until each one twinkled. He would pull my cap down over my ears for protection and hold my hand as we crossed each icy street. He would never forget to check behind me, watching for danger, on the lookout for trouble, for those who might frighten me or cause unforeseen harm.

He would want me always to be happy. It would matter when I was saddened or disheartened, even the littlest bit.

The furnace would be cranked up full blast in our basement, our house warm through and through, and the window blinds would snap up at a gentle signal, the sunset sweeping in like the cloak of a magician, transforming all shadow to golden, dark corners lit by its touch.

We would prepare for bed in a single motion, moving at the exact same pace. We would have eaten a complete dinner, and our bellies would be swollen to perfection, making us both sleepy, ready to tuck each other in.

Each night, we would lie down together, and once more read from our favorite books, this time more like singing, soft lullabies, parents gentling their children into sleep.

His head would roll back on the pillow drowsily. His eyes would close, yet I would know him not to be dead. I would understand that if I were to awaken, cold with fear in the middle of night, he would sit up without my asking. He would put his arm around my shoulder. He would whisper until I dreamed again.

If he were here, my brother,
he would love me with endurance,
and I him.

I awaken with a startle.
There is a loud rapping at the cellar door.

· DAY TEN ·

GRACE

It's still dark when Grace awakens for the last time, having drifted in and out of a restless sleep throughout the night. Finally, she can't bear lying down anymore and decides to rise. The clock by her bed says 4:00 A.M., but she knows it runs a bit fast. Surely, the detective won't call for another few hours, but she just can't stand to sit there helplessly on the corner of the bed, arms and legs crossed, trying to catch her breath and pretending that everything is all right, that Noah sleeps safely right down the hall, that it's all been just a bad dream and he'll soon awaken to eat his breakfast with her as always.

She dresses slowly, hardly noticing what she's chosen to wear, and then ties back her long curls with a tortoise-shell clip. The silver-framed photograph on the dresser glitters, and Grace reaches for it with one hand, and then watches as the small picture balanced in front falls over, then drifts to the floor.

The detective arrives by 8:00 A.M. without any news and Grace is waiting impatiently for him outside. He saunters up the front walk as if it nothing in the world is wrong and smiles at her lazily, hands in his front pants pockets.

"We think we got the sniper," he announces, "made an arrest in the middle of the night. An incredible story if you're interested, but maybe now isn't the time."

Grace feels herself swelling with fury. Why would she even care about such a thing? Doesn't he remember Noah's disappearance? Why in the world can't the police be of any help? Noah's just a boy, she thinks, biting her bottom lip. Perhaps he took the bus, then caught the train. Maybe he made it all the way to the Greyhound station and is already in another state. It wouldn't take much money for him to get far away real fast, unless he was taken, unless he's being held.

The thought of this makes it difficult for her to breathe.

But Detective Hinkle disagrees. "Where would you go," he asks her, "if you were frightened and alone? Let's take it easy now and try not to jump to conclusions. If you are correct that he was worried about the shootings and needed to disappear from sight, then I don't think he would wander aimlessly without a destination. Unless there were relatives or friends to find, but that seems not to be the case for this boy. What would you do in his situation? Would you venture out into the wide-open streets under these circumstances or would you look inward for a place to hide? I have a gut feeling that the kid might be right under our noses, although it didn't occur to me last night. Before knowing all the facts, I thought him to be a typical adolescent runaway."

"And where might 'right under our noses' be?" Grace finds it difficult to keep her irritation in check. "I've looked all over the house, even in every single closet, even under all of the beds. I can't imagine that Noah is right under our noses.

Why, I would think he'd make himself known once learning how upset I am, how much trouble he has caused. Could it be that he is just playing a silly game? I don't think so."

The detective shrugs and then starts slowly walking around the house.

"Have you checked the attic?" he asks, somewhat distracted, running his broad hand over the brick walls. She notices his nails are even, his knuckles nicked. He doesn't wear a ring.

"There isn't an attic."

Why are they wasting time with this nonsense? Does he think her stupid, a simple woman with a limited mind?

She watches as he takes a step backward, then as he looks up, shading his eyes. Once he's convinced that there's no attic structure above, he continues walking the perimeter of the house.

"You said that you looked all through the basement?" he finally asks. "You went all the way down inside? Because sometimes those in hiding can be quite clever. There have been recent situations with the police when we've missed a few obvious clues, overlooked a fugitive's hiding place ourselves."

Again, Grace is annoyed. Why is the man second-guessing her? And why are they moving so slowly, without urgency? The detective acts as if this is a minor problem, the boy's disappearance for a full eighteen hours. How can he be so relaxed, when who knows what has happened, if Noah is even still alive?

No, she won't think of that.

"There isn't any basement either, Detective Hinkle," she says evenly, trying to keep herself under control. "No attic, no basement, and the house itself is completely empty. I promise that I searched it thoroughly yesterday."

He suddenly stops dead in his tracks and then turns around. His expression's quizzical, one eyebrow raised, his mouth twisted into a frown.

"But this house was built around 1920," he says quietly, looking it over as if considering the purchase of a horse, then he runs one broad hand over its exterior, rubbing the tiny grains of dusty grout between his fingers. For a minute

Grace thinks he might put his hand to his mouth and taste the chalky stuff, as if deciding what wine to order for an evening meal.

"I guess," she replies, confused. She wonders if she's made a mistake involving this strange man; he's clearly distracted, completely on the wrong track. "But I just told you, this house doesn't have a cellar."

"Well," he continues, still staring at the walls, "all houses of this vintage have basements, even if they're just crawl spaces of some kind. It's possible that the entryway is not visible from indoors but has an exterior entrance of some sort."

She follows as he continues walking, one foot at a time, until they come to some ground cover, twisted ivy tangled in an awkward shape.

The detective stops, bends his knees, and sweeps his hand across the overgrowth. It's evident that there is some kind of clearing, an opening below, a huge plank of rotted wood. He tugs at it, then mutters something under his breath, stands and rolls up his sleeves, then bends down again.

Grace stands back as he knocks to see if the material is solid, then watches, heart beating wildly, as he pulls the door open inch by inch, until fully exposing small, narrow steps leading downward to who knows what.

He tells her to wait above, while he investigates below, but Grace can't stand the anticipation and follows his lead.

She steps down carefully behind him, holding on to his shoulder, feeling his muscles shift beneath. The light fades as they descend, and the air cools, dampens, even feels wet.

She slips suddenly, and he spins to catch her by the waist. Odd that at this peculiar moment, she observes how his arm fits perfectly around her, as if her girth is no longer gargantuan, no longer rolled with fat.

What a time to notice another's body against her own. It's been a lifetime since she let herself be held by anyone at all.

He stops short at the bottom of the stairs, and she is right behind. They both stand there for a moment, letting their eyes adjust to the light. The cellar is primitive, rough-hewn, and

Grace can hardly believe it's part of the same pristine house. The rooms upstairs are so bright and immaculate, not a crumb, not a thing out of place, while here below, just the opposite, a dark, murky space built of exposed stone, nothing but damp earth beneath her feet. She feels mud stick to her shoes and the cold creep into her bones.

But how would a boy survive here? No food, no water, no place to sleep or bathe. And as they scour every corner for evidence of life, Grace becomes more and more certain that this is a mistake, a waste of time. There's no indication of anything, of anyone hiding in this godforsaken place, this dungeon completely empty, not a sign, not a trace. And again she becomes impatient, eager to return above, to leave behind the puddles of polluted water underfoot, and the feeling of being completely lost in the dark.

The detective, however, is persistent and examines every inch of every wall. Grace finds herself exasperated. Perhaps she would have done better on her own.

And then, just as she's had enough, just as she is ready to turn herself around, she hears

Detective Hinkle call to her. He's found something, and he needs her help. His profile is invisible; he has stepped just out of her sight, and Grace stumbles forward slowly until she reaches his side.

He is crouched down near the ground with a piece of white paper in his hand. Grace can hardly believe it. Detective Hinkle holds the front page of a newspaper.

They both look down together and try to make out the date. The ink is smeared, the paper filthy, but the numbers are still discernible.

Tuesday, August 17, 2002
Hot and humid. 85–90°
Chance of thunderstorms, then clearing.

The detective puts his finger to his mouth and then points to a wooden triangle directly to their right. Grace can't imagine that it's anything significant, it's obviously too small a space, and yet here is yesterday's paper, clear as day, with the exact date.

He stands slowly and stoops so as not to

bump his head, then slides forward, all the way over to the triangular door. And then Grace can see it clearly, a splintered closet just several feet long, just several feet wide, and she is shocked when Detective Hinkle swings it open and is able to look inside.

There the boy lies, crumpled into an awkward, jumbled shape, every part of his thin body jammed tightly into the wall crevices, not an inch to spare, no room for a single other finger or toe within. Grace is immediately reminded of Pinocchio, another motherless boy, sculpted by a lonely grandfather but never really allowed his own life.

Noah's slim limbs seem wooden, perfectly still, and fold loosely from their sockets, almost appearing broken. His head dangles to one side. His skin is white, his expression frozen, as if artificially applied.

The boy rests there immobile, half dead, but she sees that he is breathing and she rushes right to his side.

His skin is cold, his face drained of color. How she wishes to hold him in her arms. But his body is so crammed into the cellar's far corner that she can barely even move his long pale hands.

"It's all right now. I'm here, Noah," she whispers into his ear. "I'll take care of you, bring you home and keep you safe. There's no need to worry anymore," she continues, stroking his cheek. "The sniper's been caught and imprisoned. No one will be hurt, no one will be shot again."

Then, to her shock and surprise, the boy moves ever so slightly in place. His eyes fly open wide for a moment; he moans softly and then faints dead away.

NOAH

Somehow, without even awakening, I know I am back in my own room, in my own bed. I sense the familiar although I don't know how.

Sometimes a body's nervous system responds to the wound by overwhelming the brain's ability to cope, causing unconsciousness.

Is it possible to be sleeping while still awake, aware of motion all around, hearing everything that is being said, every last sound, and that I am languishing in some kind of feverish dream, at home but still somewhere far off, under my covers yet observing from above? My eyes are closed and still I see colors, shapes swirling all about, and hear her voice surrounding me, warm, peaceful, full of grace.

She sits waiting, never leaving my side, and I listen to her speaking to another. A man answers from way over there. Each voice is tossed back and forth as if in a game of catch, just missing my long bed.

Her words are gentle, soft and wide, while his are louder: they echo and boom.

Thank you for coming back. I know it's late.

No matter. I wanted to. Sorry it took so long, but it's been really crazy downtown. How is the boy, any change?

No, nothing, and I'm worried. It's midnight, and he's still asleep. Will he be okay? Do you think everything will be all right?

Yes, of course, I'm sure, but you should get some rest yourself. Do you want me to sit with him for a spell, while you take a break and lie down?

No, thank you. I want to stay, be here when he wakes, but are you sure we shouldn't call a doctor? After all, it's been so long that the boy has been asleep.

Not yet, let's just wait and see. It's only

natural that he would be exhausted. Rest is prob-
ably the best cure.

Two voices, two halves, together yet apart.
Identical in every aspect, joined at the heart,
victim and villain,
guard and prisoner,
one lucid, one possibly insane,
survivor and sacrificial lamb.

He's so pale, his skin feels cold.
That's only normal after losing conscious-
ness the way he did.
That was hours ago, and still . . .
But remember, it's been a while for him in
that cellar, not much to eat or drink—no wonder
he's tired and weak. Just try to let him be. It's just
after twelve now, it has been a good amount of
time. He'll come to soon. Don't worry, give him
a little while. I checked his vitals before, when we
found him, and everything seems just fine. His
pulse was a bit accelerated, but it should slow
down again soon.
He's gone through so much, my poor boy. And

the shock of it all, I guess it takes a terrible toll. The loss of his grandmother's companionship, which he's never really dealt with, and all the shootings. It's just too much for someone of his age.

A thin boy's shadow flickers, then evaporates. Look, he was just there, over that hillside. I promise. I saw him move . . . and then vanish soundlessly into thin air.

Where did he go, now that I can't find him, now that I don't have a reason for him to exist? And where is he now, if not out there wildly shooting at the hard-hearted world? Where has he been all of this time—camouflaged, hiding in foxholes, responsible for all of our crimes?

There was a voice without a body, entreating, calling out my name, knocking without interruption at my own heart's door.

Have I been solitary all along, separate, only one and never two?

Could it be that for all these years I have actually been untwinned, two sides of the same person, already whole?

The sound of a cricket's harsh chirping in my

ear, the brush of its fragile body, how it quickly
disappears.

How old is the boy? He looks so young.
Just thirteen.
Who'll care for him when you leave? Are
there any relatives, any family at all around?
No. No one, no one. That's the problem. He's
lived here with his grandmother since he was just
a little boy, and there is apparently no one, no one
else to step into his life and help right now.

My covers are floating, my bed in midair, and
my heart also rises, separate, a compact body of
its own. It has the oddest color, both black and
blue, as if beaten and made swollen by invisible
fists. I try to call out to it: "Stop that roaming,
come back where you belong," but it swings from
my bedroom ceiling, not a part of me at all.

Perhaps this is what they mean by the word
heartless. Someone who has lost everything, even
his very own insides, that muscle beating rebel-
liously somewhere else outside.

·   ·   ·

Shh, maybe he's waking. Look how he's turning his head. Do you think he can hear us, will he recognize his name? Noah, it's me, Grace, sitting here by your side. Look at me, say something, so that I'll know you're okay.

Maybe a drink of water, something cold to bring him to. Do you want me to get him a glass from downstairs, so you can stay and be here if he wakes?

Yes, thank you. I appreciate it. You're being so kind. Are you sure it is all right that you're taking off from work? I really hate to impose. After all, you've given us so much of your time. I mean, it won't be a problem to be away from the station when so much is going on right now?

No, don't give it a thought. Right now, anyway, I'm on my way home. It's been a long day on all fronts, both here and at work. Besides, I hate to leave you alone—you look a bit shaken up yourself.

I suppose this boy's really gotten to me, somehow left a mark. I just don't know how I'll be able to leave him, at least without being sure that he'll be all right.

·   ·   ·

This room is filled with people, a kind woman, a man, and a sleeping boy. When will he awaken, when will his body be reunited with its organs, his heart with his mind? I watch him, confused, recognizing his familiar shattered shape, and wish that he would remember how to speak, how to ask for her help. What if he stays there forever, half dead, half alive, and won't be able to thank her for her understanding, her willingness to pursue him through thick and through thin?

The air blows, then settles, as if from outdoors. Perhaps now he will be able to float down below to be with the others.

But how his pillow is drenched, it is soaked through and through.

Of course, he is crying, just a broken-hearted little boy, and someone's hand is at his neck, her arms hold him tight.

There is a ribbon of human tissue cordoning off this room. It winds tight and tighter, bringing them closer and closer.

They sit face-to-face, bound together and yet

loose, still breathing on their own while sharing the same heart.

When I think of this moment later, I will remember her long, soft hair, how my cheek pressed against her collar, the weave of its fabric leaving my face creased. And when I look at myself in the mirror, later that night, this mark is still visible, perhaps even permanent, left there for all time.

"I know that you're very tired, Noah," Grace says later that afternoon when I have had time to rest and regain most of my strength. We are sitting together at the kitchen table, face-to-face. Although she had offered to bring me up a tray in the exact manner Mademoiselle took her meals, I declined her offer, preferring to go downstairs. My footsteps were wobbly, but I was careful not to trip, and Grace walked right beside me so that I could lean on her when I tired.

Grace pours me a cup of my favorite green tea, and I notice a few curls of auburn hair, perhaps dampened by the humid kitchen air, curling around her neck like a baby's soft ringlets.

"I really don't want to press you, Noah, after going through so much. But I do wonder why you found it necessary to leave the way you did, and want to know if I did something to upset you, or if it was just all the shootings and, of course, your grandmother. Maybe now that the violence is over and the service arranged, you might finally be ready to face and talk about things."

I can see that Grace is somehow uncharacteristically nervous. She hides her mouth with one hand and, for a moment, glances down, a mannerism I have not noticed before. Could it be that she feels responsible for my departure and running away from home? How could she know that my leaving had nothing to do with her at all? I resist the temptation to tell her everything that has been on my mind for so long.

She looks up at me carefully, waiting for a response.

I shrug and take a sip of tea, still burning hot. I do not answer. I do not have anything to say.

"It's time," she continues slowly. "It's time for you to look up at me and finally face your situation head-on."

I close my eyes and inhale. The cup is shaking in my hand.

"Noah, we both know that you can't put it off any longer. You can't go on pretending and covering up the hurt."

I nod, but do not mean to. Then I speak without saying anything at all. I feel my lips tremble and start the sentence I have avoided for so long.

She waits patiently. Even the air is still.

"Should I say it for you?"

I shake my head. They are my words to speak, my life, my grandmother and my twin.

She tilts her face toward me. I see a reddish flicker of her hair. Her hand on my arm, then holding my hand tight.

"Mademoiselle," I begin slowly, "my grandmother, is not upstairs."

"And?"

"She never came home from the hospital. She never will."

Neither of us speaks for a moment and I feel the whoosh of summer air. Grace has left the window open, the kitchen filling with sudden warmth. We both turn to look for the source, but of course there is nothing to be seen. Just an ordinary open window and the pale green leaves of a nearby tree.

"Is that why you left?" Grace asks me quietly. "Is that why you decided to suddenly run away?"

I shake my head, then nod. "Partly," I whisper. "Maybe partly that and more."

"The upcoming memorial? Were you worried about that, and all the terrible shootings—did all of that have you scared?"

How do I answer such questions? How do I explain my peculiar fear? How to tell Grace about my birth, my twin, the surgery, the crime of separation? How to reveal all of that?

I think not.

In any case, in light of the recent arrest, my concerns are clearly unfounded, even ridiculous. What made me make these outlandish assumptions in the first place? Why did such thoughts even take root?

I will not respond to Grace—some things are simply not to be discussed—so I give her an incomplete answer, both false and true at the same time, but also one that I am certain she will be sure to understand.

"I guess," I finally say. The tea leaves a sweet taste on my tongue, but its heat has burned the roof of my mouth, making it somewhat difficult to speak. "Everything, all together, had me a little worried and confused. I suppose I just felt a little desperate, and had to get away for a while. I don't know, I guess I was not thinking clearly, but I'm sorry for the trouble that I have caused."

Grace smiles and pours yet another cup of tea.

"Don't worry about that," she says quietly. "I'm just glad that you are home safe and sound and that the police finally caught the sniper. Actually, it's quite surprising, bizarre and very strange—it turns out that the shooter is a woman, not a man, as everyone first thought. And, believe it or not, this troubled soul is a mother who dragged around her poor teenage daughter, also forcing the child to do harm. The papers say the two are practically identical, although of course years apart, and they disguised themselves to look like two young boys. Apparently, the daughter had a terrible deformity, born without a normal face, her features all jumbled together, pretty hideous and frightening I guess, the disfigurement monstrous, impossible to improve or fix with surgery. And of course the kids at her school teased her unmercifully, never giving the poor girl a chance, making her into an outcast, she and the mother both. I guess the deformity was a birth defect from some kind of medicine improperly prescribed during the mom's pregnancy—I think I've heard about a similar condition before. In any case, it seems that both the girl and her mother had been planning to take their own lives after acting out their horrific rage.

"Can you imagine such anger against humanity, such bitterness against the world? I feel so sorry for both of them, particularly the child."

I shrug. I can imagine. I can picture it all. But I also know the murders are over and that there is no need to be frightened anymore. But even so, my hands quiver slightly, and then begin to shake—the thought of Mademoiselle's imminent service inconceivable. I know that she has passed, but still think of her as alive, and cannot conceive of having the strength to make it all the way through a final good-bye. What if I lose control completely and break down into tears? What if I faint dead away and cannot be revived?

"Noah, you know that I'll be there with you," Grace says gently, as if reading my mind. "We will be together for the entire day. You won't have to be alone."

Her eyes fill up for a moment, and I hope she doesn't cry.

"Mademoiselle would have liked tulips," I finally hear myself say, "yellow and red. Those were her favorite flowers, and I would appreciate it if we could have them at the service, if that is possible at all."

Graces smiles again, and then pats me softly on the hand.

"Why do you always refer to your grandmother as Mademoiselle?" she asks, as if hearing it for the first time. "I've always wondered, and have meant to ask you about that for a long while now."

I shrug. I do not answer. I am busing chewing my food.

"Most kids would call her grandma, right?"

I shrug again, and look down at the food on

my plate. A grilled chicken sandwich, corn chips, macaroni salad mixed with green peppers and slices of boiled egg. The bread is whole wheat, filled with the tiniest of seeds, and they crunch in my mouth, making a comforting sound.

"I always knew her as Mademoiselle," I finally reply, "from the beginning, from when I was small, and never called her by anything else. And she hated the term 'grandmother'—she said that would not do at all."

"But why 'Mademoiselle'? Why that particular name?"

"I guess because it was her stage name, at least that's what she told me a long time ago. She was called Mademoiselle when she was a young working girl. My grandmother was an entertainer, a dancer back then, actually quite famous in the days of vaudeville. Her professional stage name was Mademoiselle du Coeur Manqué, and I guess she just shortened it to one word."

Grace looks thoughtful for a moment and offers a plate of small chocolate almond cakes. She is wearing a pink flowered blouse with wide caftan sleeves that expose her sturdy arms all the way up to her elbows. The bones at her wrists are prominent, bulky and thick, reminding me of some kind of structure bolted together with steel. I notice a streak of chocolate on her right palm.

"I know how much you cared for her, what a good grandson you always were, but did you ever wonder about how well she took care of you, how she might have given you more attention when you were growing up?"

"But it was she who needed help," I say, piling my plate with two desserts, one to eat now and one for later, when I still may be starved.

I am beginning to feel a bit anxious, not sure if I want to talk about this at all. My grandmother would not have wanted her personal life discussed.

"It was my grandmother who was the weaker. She was the delicate one," I add hesitantly. "She needed to be cared for, to be looked after. It was she who required more, not me at all. Sometimes it is necessary to sacrifice so that someone you love can survive."

I feel my heart both softening and hardening at the same time. Strange to be talking about Mademoiselle out loud in this way. I am not used to discussing her past, how she lived, how she treated me. I am not used to sharing with anyone what has always been so private before.

"But don't you understand, Noah, that it wasn't your job to care for her in this way? No matter how much you loved her. You needed care yourself—a child deserves to be loved and cherished. Protected. It's a privilege to be able to care for a young boy. You weren't protected when you needed it the most, and I'm not sure that someone your age should have to give up so much for anyone, relative or not."

I gulp. "She took me in when there was no one, my only living family member—she told me that herself. There was no one else who wanted me."

"She told you that?"

"Yes."

"And you loved her."

"I did."

"You wanted what was best for her."

"Yes."

"Well, from my point of view, I think maybe you were asked to give too much, to sacrifice too much of your own wants and needs. I don't mean to put down your grandmother, or not give her the proper respect. She was obviously quite a lady, and provided you a home for a long time. But what about you, Noah, what about your own wishes and desires? Weren't they important too? Didn't you ever want something different for yourself, something more? Weren't you ever resentful, angry about being left so much on your own? Any child deserves better, no matter what the situation."

I shrug.

"You know," Grace says gently, noticing my hands clenched together as if in prayer, "it's all right if you resent your grandmother a little, it's okay to be angry about the situation, about the way you were raised. It doesn't mean that you don't love her deeply for the woman that she was, but maybe you had a right to expect something else from your own childhood."

I feel my shoulder bones clatter.

How does Grace know so much about my childhood, my past, my personal life? I find myself uncomfortable with what feels like prying, despite my appreciation of her help, and simply don't wish to discuss it anymore. But I try not to withdraw silently, the way I have always done before, and tell her quietly that the subject of Mademoiselle is off limits for now.

I'm sure she understands, because she changes the topic right away, and we sit there for a long while, eating chocolate cakes and drinking sweet green tea.

But later that night, as I pass my Mademoiselle's closed door, I think of how much I actually do miss her, her odd, eccentric ways, just knowing that she was lying there in the next room all those years, someone who was a blood relative, who claimed me as her own.

Knowing that she was always right there in her bedroom, even if existing in a kind of half life, reassured me greatly as a child, and somehow kept an important part of me alive.

And yet I think about what Grace has said of childhood, about love and sacrifice, and wonder if it was fair that I never had much of a normal life. Did I deserve better? Was there something else to be had?

Maybe Grace is correct about resentment,

about what my real feelings are. But emotions aren't my strong point, and I am used to keeping them at arm's length. I turn around and walk back to Mademoiselle's room, but I do not muster the courage to open her door, and wonder if I will ever be able to go inside again.

Will her bed be just as I left it the day she was to come home? Will her dressing table be in the same corner, the chaise placed at the exact same angle as before? Will her silk robe still be hanging on the inside of the closet door? Will her dresses be lined up as always, like headless bodies hanging covered in knotted plastic bags?

Will her jewelry be hidden, forbidden sweets in the secret velvet-lined drawer?

Will the bottle be under her pillow? Will there be others stuffed behind the heavy draperies?

Will her body still be outlined on her bed?

Or has all of this somehow been altered by time?

I pretended to myself that she would once again return, even though the doctor had already called from the hospital with the unfortunate news, even though Grace also called to let me know she would be my day-care provider, even though I actually knew the whole truth.

What lingers inside my grandmother's room that still frightens and worries me so? I'm not sure, but for now, I will not think about it anymore.

It is still early in the evening, but I am extremely tired and worn, every muscle aching, my whole body ready for bed. But when I lie down and reach for something inviting to read, the books on my shelves stretch their gleaming spines in unison, and then breathe out again, exhaling their stories, some forgotten, some remembered.

All of the reading I have done over my thirteen years of life suddenly takes on a shape and meaning not previously understood. And a host of questions occur to me, never posed before: Why have I spent so much of my life with these books? What is their significance, their power? Why give yourself over to such a variety of characters, to different plots and themes, if not to learn something about yourself, gain insight, change and grow?

In the past, I have used reading to escape

from my own life, and now I must reconsider, find myself in each and every tale.

Then I watch, stunned and amazed. All my books, thick ones, thin ones, hardback and paper, old and new, fly open all together, as if touched by a wand, and I see the words on white pages arch their curved little backs and raise their tiny black hands.

They all point in the same direction, a clearing up ahead.

And then all at once I can see what was never visible before. It is as if I suddenly have supernatural powers. X-ray vision, an ability to look right through the frigid haze that has for so long drifted through this little frozen house.

My twin is not out there waiting, crazed with anger and revenge; he does not wander restlessly outside my small universe, neglected, longing to be allowed in.

It is only me, Noah, this abandoned, pitiful boy, who has stumbled through a cold, cold house, forever bewildered and ignored. It has been my own bottomless fury that has shadowed me about, my own yearning that called out desperately, a pathetic whimpering craving to be heard.

I have been the exiled specter, grotesque and shunned by the world, limping pitifully through life as if crippled, my nose pressed against the window, my shoulder at the door.

Perhaps there is no such thing as perfect doubles, identical twins forever conjoined, interchangeable souls.

Maybe just one is enough to be whole.

I close my eyes, and then I hear Grace's gentle voice, something about not having to sacrifice everything of your own for someone else, not even for a grandmother whom you might love very much indeed.

"Mademoiselle didn't really love me, did she?" I ask Grace out of the blue that evening, when washing dishes after dinner, feeling my throat fill up so it is almost impossible to speak. "If she loved me, then she wouldn't have left me so alone."

"But she did, Noah." Grace stops stacking the dishes and looks directly at me, without blinking an eye. "She must have. She loved you in the only way she knew how. But love is complicated, and doesn't always take one form."

I stop to think of this now, the heart's irregular shape, the way Mademoiselle loved inconsistently, how her touch was completely unfamiliar, how she never hugged or kissed me, how she never exhibited any affection at all.

How she drank herself to sleep each night, how she never stirred when I was ill, never rose to make my breakfast, how she never offered me much of herself at all. How she turned away when I needed her, how I lived for years as if alone, how I watched her disease take over, left behind to my own woeful resources before I could even understand what they were.

She was my grandmother and my responsibility.

She made me a parent when I should have remained a child.

But I also remember Mademoiselle when I was much younger, those first years after I arrived as a young boy in her home. Her days in bed were fewer then, and I even recall her picking me up after school. She was always the one dressed most fancifully, usually wearing some broad-brimmed, feathered hat. Her dress would be a bright color, her shoes and purse always matching, her lipstick *Masquerade Red*.

I would drop whatever I was doing and run straight to her, then watch as she tottered backward on high heels. She would smile at me quizzically and wave with a tentative, gloved hand as if surprised to encounter someone unknown yet familiar, as if meeting her grandson for the first time.

She always smelled of something sweet, yet also rancid—her breath, even then, was sour. I remember her leaning toward me, and the small puff of cold vapor from her mouth.

For my afternoon snack she used to bring me street-vendor chestnuts wrapped in a handkerchief embroidered with her name. We would rub their ridged shells with our fingernails until they cracked and split open in our hands. But their flesh was often inedible, scorched through and through, and it always confused me how something burned so completely could still be so perfectly cold.

"What a shame, my dear." Mademoiselle would smile, unflustered. "I guess I have kept them in my purse for too long. Let's see what I can find you in the kitchen cupboards. Perhaps we can make some lunch when we get home."

But we would both forget this intention, once we finally made it through the front door. Instead, I would bring my grandmother her favorite silk bathrobe and watch her fall asleep on the petite chaise lounge.

And soon those days were numbered, and it wasn't long until she took to her bed. I was a child taught to comfort an aging grandmother and to pretend that everything was normal, that I had no need to be nourished or cared for, no right even to be fed.

She referred to me as "dear" and "darling," but then quickly looked away. She drank and hid the bottles from sight, but not from observation; she slept through most of every day.

> She never checked my homework.
> She never cared about my books.
> She never called me by my given name.
> She never knew who I really was,
> my dreams, my needs, my wants.

I still miss her desperately and long to see her again.

Hearts can be different shapes and sizes, some barely recognizable at all.

· DAY ELEVEN ·

GRACE

Grace sits by Noah's bed hour after hour, staring at his little pinched face, the delicate necklace of sweat around his neck and the purplish veins that tremble at the inside of his long, thin wrists. What if he sleeps forever; what if he never wakes?

What was it she had learned about coma and traumatic injury at the hospital just two years ago? Waiting in the hallway, the doctor had looked down at her as he spoke, white flecks of spittle at the corners of his mouth sucked in and out with every word. Her mother didn't even rise from the plastic corridor chair, her head hung down low.

"Coma as a result of comprehensive trauma is always difficult to assess. The first twenty-four hours are critical, but after that we should know more. Take this pamphlet, why don't you—it may help you better understand what your brother is up against. The medical profession uses a standard system of scoring trauma when attempting to assess damage. Take a look at it while you're waiting—you might want to read it along with the boy's mother, you know, in order to prepare."

He coughed and snuffled, taking two small steps back.

Her heart shrunk, then shriveled, then evaporated into smoke.

"Over there is a waiting room." He pointed to several more chairs and a television, its small screen flickering blank. "Make yourself comfortable and we will be sure to let you know if anything changes at all."

Comfortable? The man was clearly out of his mind.

His pale mask hung from his neck like a twin face, featureless, yet imprinted with the mold of his sharp nose, a long mouth. His jacket was white, with a plastic tag printed in black.

GERALD ROTH, M.D.
INTENSIVE CARE, PEDIATRICS

Who cared what his name was? He didn't matter at all.

But if he had intensive care to provide, could he please offer it now?

She had looked down quickly at the paper in her hand. Each word hurt to read, then whizzed through her like a bullet, settling in her cavernous, empty chest.

Now, sitting here with another boy, she remembers it all.

TRAUMA SCORING
(Score from 1–5, 5 being the best)
Best Eye Response
1. no eye opening
2. eye opening to pain
3. eye opening to verbal command

Best Verbal Response
1. no verbal response
2. incomprehensible sounds
3. inappropriate words
4. confused
5. orientated

Best Motor Response

1. no motor response
2. extension to pain
3. withdrawal from pain
4. localized pain
5. obeys command

How would Grace score Noah now?

No eye opening. No verbal response. No motor response.

In fact, how would she score herself in regard to trauma?

Eyes closed to the truth. Confused. Withdrawal from pain.

Her score would be worse than the boy's.

Suddenly, to her surprise, Noah moans and opens his eyes. Suddenly he is crying in her arms, the first time he has permitted her to come near, much less hug him, draw him close. She wishes they could sit there together forever, just the two of them, not speaking, not even saying a single word. She may have made her mistakes, but there is one thing she is absolutely certain of, one thing she knows for sure—when it comes to the soothing of the injured, Grace knows what she is doing: she is able to make the hurt less painful, to begin the healing of wounds.

She doesn't care what her supervisor would say if she knew, or about the day-care provider rules and regulations about boundaries. Grace already knows how to tend to a young boy.

She knows just how to give comfort to a child.

Just let me, just let me, just let me help.

And for a short while, he does just that. He lets her, and she feels her own heart strengthen, become muscular, grow.

· DAY TWELVE ·

NOAH

This morning, we find the thermostat together.

Grace says, "Can you believe it, Noah, after freezing in here day after day! It's been in front of our noses all this time."

We are standing by the oven, checking to see if the cranberry scones are done, when my pants catch on something sharp, a nail of some kind. And when I crouch down to examine the damage, to see if the tear can be sewn, I notice a little tiny dial at the corner of my thumb. Right under the ledge of the kitchen cabinet, a most peculiar place to hang, it glitters in the morning light, and for a minute I can't see much of anything at all. Then Grace bends down alongside me and follows my eyes ahead: we walk our fingers up the cabinet paneling, ten tiny climbers crawling a steep mountain cliff.

The silver numbers are suddenly illuminated, as if lit by a small bulb inside, and the temperature is as we thought, set extremely low. Grace and I look at one another, and without saying a single word, together we move the dial all the way up.

Our hands touch briefly, one layering the other, then slowly separate. We both sit down on the floor, thoroughly pleased. The plastic thermostat cover is transparent, and it is easy to see the small numbers move. Up and up the small red arrow floats, until it reaches seventy degrees, and then we both sigh. We are content with this outcome, not too warm, but not the least bit cold. We nod at each other and soundlessly shake hands.

I reach out to help her stand up, but she flounders for a minute below, too large to rise entirely on her own. Then I stumble also, having nothing solid to grab. The kitchen cupboard drawers slide open when I reach for them, and the oven handle is already loose, unable to bear any consequential weight. I look over at Grace for a moment, her face flushed with the effort of trying to stand by herself, and for a moment I am reminded of myself, stubborn, determined, doing everything on my own.

The kitchen floor is slippery, a slick linoleum tile, and Grace and I will need to hold on to each other tightly if we want to be sure not to fall.

It is not long before the house begins to warm up. Funny, but I cannot remember a time, spring, summer, winter, or fall, that I did not need to wear long sleeves, or even a warm sweater inside. Suddenly all that is changed, and in the middle of the afternoon, when Grace and I are discussing the evening dinner, I realize that I am uncomfortably warm, even hot.

"An Italian recipe," Grace says absentmindedly when she notices me staring at the red splatters on her shirt. "Lasagna, one of my favorite dishes. I haven't had it for years and thought it might be good for dinner tonight."

I shrug. Oddly enough, I have never eaten this particular dish, and although I know it to be fairly common, I am not exactly sure what it is. Suddenly, the thought of a large plate of hot food for dinner makes me feel queasy. For some reason I don't have much of an appetite today.

"You know," I say slowly, rolling up my shirt sleeves in an effort to cool off, "I'm not sure that I'm really up for such a big meal tonight. Do you think that we could just have a sandwich or something light?"

I am uneasy about disappointing Grace, about interfering with her plans, but at the same time I feel compelled to speak my mind.

"Why, certainly, Noah. Of course." She smooths the wrinkles on her left sleeve and looks me dead in the eye. "Are you feeling well? You're awfully quiet this afternoon."

"I'm fine," I reply, but find myself shaking my head at the same time.

"Worried about the day after tomorrow?"

Yes. Worried and more. But I don't really want to think about it now. I don't really want to tell.

"Noah?"

"No, I'm fine," I repeat. "I don't know, I'm just not really that hungry. Maybe it's the heat."

Ever since we altered the thermostat, the house's temperature has significantly changed, and I suppose that, while it is definitely a relief, such a drastic difference requires some adjustment. I'm not exactly a boy used to sudden changes, and there seem to have been quite a few in recent days.

"Well," Grace says, snapping the cookbook shut, "perhaps we set the temperature too high too quickly. Perhaps you're not used to the warmth as yet—it may take some time to acclimate. But we can easily readjust the setting if you like. This is your house, and it's your call."

"No, it's okay, really. Maybe it's not the heat, maybe . . ."

"Yes?" She stares at me intently, chin on her hand, elbow on the table, as if I am the only important thing in the whole world.

"Have you ever been to a funeral or memorial service before? I mean, I guess you probably have been to quite a few in your life, but I have not."

Grace's lip seems to tremble for a moment and she looks down. Her long, wavy hair, usually held back with clips, falls forward over her face like a veil, and then back again as she raises her face to me.

"Yes," she says slowly. "I have."

She takes a clip from her pocket and secures her hair in a loose knot at the nape of her neck.

"Will I have to say anything?"

"Not if you don't want to."

I am silent for a moment. I try to imagine what she might have looked like at the time of her final hour, my grandmother, my Mademoiselle, lying immobile, alone on a hospital bed, her eyes wide open, her thin mouth forming a surprised O. I cringe and look down. Why torture myself with such details? I must learn not to let my imagination take hold.

"No," I finally say softly. "At the service, I would prefer not to say a word."

Grace nods.

"Anything else?" she asks. "Any other wishes or concerns?"

"Who else will be there? At the ceremony."

"We won't really know until we get there. Perhaps some of your grandmother's old acquaintances. Perhaps some of her friends. Maybe some people you don't even know. All family and known acquaintances have been notified."

What family? Which acquaintances?

"Oh," I say. "Oh."

I am not eager for Grace to know how alone we were, Mademoiselle and me, how there really is no one else at all.

"And Detective Hinkle. He asked if he could attend. In fact, he was nice enough to offer us a ride. Would that be okay with you?"

I nod.

"Noah?"

I nod again.

"We haven't talked about after, have we? We haven't discussed what will happen after all of this is over. Where you will live, where I will go."

"Later," I say, sliding my chair back from the table. "I don't want to talk about any of that now."

"Okay. But I want you to know that no matter what, no matter what happens afterward, I'll always be available to you."

Sure. Right. How?

But I don't say any of that. I don't really want to have this conversation or hear Grace's assurances anymore. I don't want to think about tomorrow or the day after that or the day after that. I would just prefer that everything remain the same for a while to come. Grace living here with me, our cooking, reading, and playing Scrabble together. Our knowing how to keep each other company and also how to leave each other alone. Why is that too much to ask?

But no, it is too much, and things will not be the same at all. The day after tomorrow will come with all of its unavoidable finality. I will have to say good-bye to all of them, to the imagined life of my brother, my twin; to my grandmother, my Mademoiselle; and to Grace, my friend.

And then she will leave.

No matter what she says to me now, no matter what she wants, I will be alone. There will be nobody else, nobody else for me at all. Once more I will be forced to separate, divided in half.

No use to pretend otherwise any longer. Not all that different from before, anyway—not that different at all.

From the beginning, ever since that fateful day, I have always been by myself. It is time to acknowledge this now.

I must face the true history of my own life.

Nobody wanted either of us to die, but a terrible decision had to be made on that dreadful day.

One or the other, not both.

Some of the doctors even broke down and cried.

Mademoiselle once told me this, and I remember it now.

They washed their hands and stood waiting, palms raised, as if to indicate each one of them was weaponless, that they all came in peace.

Masks covered their faces, sky-blue caps on their heads.

They could see only one another's eyes, the rest of their features were disguised.

Magnetic imaging had been completed beforehand, but no one really knew what to expect once inside.

The first incision was made in the afternoon.

Twenty-two surgeons and nurses tended to us then.

With infinite tenderness they took turns cutting through gossamer skin and delicate bone, layer by layer.

Carving with an impeccable touch.

They whispered to one another. Someone hummed.

They had to work slowly.

At times there was a tangle of hands.

A sponge bounced, and then fell to the floor.

The glittering instruments cauterized our tiny vessels and sealed off each minuscule cut.

There was almost no bleeding at all.

Our reflexes were tested again and again, stimulating bits of shimmering nerve.

Each time we were touched, we sparkled, shuddering.

Once and then twice.

At eight hours they carefully opened the membranes that wrapped around our spines like a twist of miniature hands.

Then they closed them once more.

Next, the internal organs were divided, one by one.

Did we feel anything? Did our little heart skip a beat?

At sixteen hours, the only attachment was that of blood vessels, the pathway of our lives.

When they were cut, one would soon die.

The ultimate sacrifice.

Additional surgery was necessary for the survivor then: the diaphragm, chest, and abdominal wall were calling for immediate attention, comprehensive repair.

Reconstruction is difficult, a procedure really never complete.

The wounds were large, requiring an intricate stitch.

Some of them still need closing.

And now, the question remains, whom should be chosen to live and whom to die, and exactly why?

Was his sacrifice necessary for my salvation, and how was the stronger determined, the one with greater potential for life?

Should separation have ever taken place?

Should we have been allowed to die together in each other's arms?

And who has the right to choose who is taken and who remains?

But the truth must be told, my own past faced.

We were separated out of love and kindness, not because of hate.

I will think of how gently he was let go, instead of embalming my brother with bitterness and rage.

But do I have to recall all of this, dwell on all of it right now? I think not. I don't have the energy or will.

Perhaps later today, or perhaps tomorrow, I will climb the steep stairs all the way to my bedroom. Maybe I will lie down for a rest, maybe I will read one of my books for a while, maybe I will retrieve my scrapbook from inside the closet and look at it all over again.

I will begin on page one.

Maybe I will pull up the Private Box of the Invisible Boy from under the floorboards. Maybe this time I will take off the heavy lid.

I have never done that before.

Magnetic imaging is not necessary to know what will be found inside.

An infinitesimal lock of downy hair, a delicate footprint the size of a fingernail, the transparent bracelet from his wrist, too small, too fragile, for the imprint of any particular name.

Identification was never a problem, although we looked just the same.

He was the one not able to breathe on his own.

He had difficulty sucking and opening his little eyes.

His life depended on my heart pumping for us both; he had no strength of his own, and his mind was curdled, undeveloped, so I'm told.

His lungs were weak.

He faltered while I did not.

They say the newborn don't see, but I remember this:

Your eyelids were ruffled.
I think you whimpered once, a crumpled cough,
then opened your tiny mouth again

dribbling pretty foam.
Your breath was embalmed with milk:
    sticky sweet.

You saw me too.

"Noah?"
I look up.
She leans toward me, her brow furrowed, concern written all over her face.
"Noah?"
I love the way Grace says my name. With a lilt in her voice. Tentatively, as if always asking the same question over and over again.
Noah, are you all right?
Noah, is there something you need?
Noah, do you know I am here?
Noah, do you believe I care?
Do I believe? I'm not sure.
"Noah, I promise you."
I look up at her, then turn away. It is somehow difficult to look right into her face.
"Can I tell you a secret? Something nobody else can know?"

I nod.

She leans toward me and the dusty air between us glistens. I smell a hint of citrus, maybe lemon, on her breath. Then a sudden whiff of something else—sweeter, lavender or rose petal—wafting up from a loose strand of long, shiny hair.

"There once was another," she says softly, almost in a whisper, "and I cared for him very deeply. And I suppose my work will give me the opportunity to get to know many other children, at least that's what I hope. But I don't think there will be another quite like you, Noah. You will always have a place in my life."

I feel my skin prickle and I blink. It is as if someone has shone a light right into my eyes.

"This might not be very professional of me," Grace continues, "and I know that I shouldn't speak my mind, but I really want you to know how I feel. You are a very special boy, and I have no intention of ever forgetting you, or of ever not being a part of your future. I'm not exactly sure what that means right now—I may not be able to live here with you again, but I will tell you this:

I will never disappear from your life, and you will always be a part of mine."

I look up at her now. Are those tears in her eyes?

Is it possible that what I have wished for has come true?

Is it possible for half a boy's heart to be whole?

Grace's face is round, her skin glossy. Her mouth widens into a miraculously large smile, and I can't remember seeing a face stretch open so far, as if her skin is filament, composed of light rather than simple human cells.

Her cheeks are full, flushed sunrise pink, and a few loose threads from her yellow collar flutter at her chin like miniature butterflies. I close my eyes for a moment, her colors so bright that it almost hurts to look, almost overwhelming to see, as if I have just come out of a darkened room into broad daylight.

I look closer.

Hers is a wide nose, soft and round, no hard edges, and covered with a dusting of copper freckles. The dappled skin under her eyes, two small, upside-down arcs, are like tiny rowboats, the mix of colors iridescent as a rainbow. And when she smiles, as she is doing now, the far corners drift upward ever so slightly, as if she is both amused and concerned at the same time.

Now she is nodding, as if to answer a question, and the very ends of her thick red curls, knotted at her neck in a bun, loosen, crackling in the dry air.

Somehow, I am embarrassed. I turn my head away.

"Look at me, Noah," she says. Her lips are full, chapped. There is a tiny oblong scar at one corner as if she had been burned while eating.

My hands are crossed on my lap. I watch them tremble. Slowly, as if lifted by a string, one palm is raised, the fingers curled, then straighten.

She is reaching out her own hand to mine, her fingertips square, the nails chipped, uneven, her whole hand so full of flesh it wobbles, wide, thick, almost liquid, no bones there.

I have never seen anything more beautiful, my guardian, my secret twin.

"This has been a cold house," I say.

"Yes."

She takes my thin hand in her own.

A jolt, a spark, slices between us—an electrical shock from the carpet below—and we both laugh, loosen our grip, and then hold on tightly again.

My skin warms to her touch, but my bones still rattle, feel brittle, and I see my entire hand disappear in her broad palm.

I am suddenly afraid. There is so little of me as it is. I can't afford to lose more.

But her hand tightens around mine, and I can see that she has no intention of letting me go.

"Now that you are not alone," she says quietly, almost in a hoarse whisper, "and before the day of the service arrives, I think it's time you come to terms with all that has happened. I think it's time to open your grandmother's door."

I shiver and hear something inside me murmur, but cannot quite understand what is being said.

She cocks her head to one side. A long curl loosens and wiggles from its clasp as if something alive.

Once I saw a dog, a retriever of some kind,

in a documentary on TV giving birth.

"Look at that," Mademoiselle had said. "Only one born alive? The others must be deformed, dead inside the womb. Such a paltry litter seems unnatural, doesn't it, my dear? Do you know, some animals actually eat their newborns, ingest the little beasts from head to toe? Oh, birth is so often full of pain and dread, my darling; in fact it's quite disturbing, not worth the suffering or tribulation. Turn the channel, why don't you, dear. I don't care to watch this show anymore."

How unkind that was, I think to myself now. That was a mean thing for Mademoiselle to say. It is even more unnatural for a grandmother to swallow a small boy whole.

"I can't," I finally say to Grace. 'I won't."

"Yes." She squeezes my hand tighter. "You can. You must. And if you like, I will come with you."

And so we walk together, Grace and I, silently up the stairs, my heart tumbling, beating so loudly that I want to cover both ears.

I will shut my eyes. I will not look at all.

But when the door swings open slowly, when the familiar scents drift toward me, I forget this promise and drop Grace's hand.

Face cream, lipstick, and sweet sherry.
Hair spray, perfume, whisky, and mint.
Laundry starch, air freshener, and nail polish.
Witch hazel and gin.

I rush over to my grandmother's empty bed and kneel beside it.
The duvet cover is folded just as I had left it, the blankets tucked in, her tiny pointed black satin slippers neatly arranged on the floor.
I am weeping.
The bed's stiff dust ruffle scratches my face, and then suddenly wilts.
I am certain that Mademoiselle would not have approved.

GRACE

There would be one more game of Scrabble to play before her departure.

She sits next to Noah on the living room couch, the blue, purple, and pink checkered board spread out on the coffee table before them, a plate of raspberry angel food cake balancing on the cushion in between. The confection towers tall and cylindrical, having been baked in a deep double-dish Bundt pan, and it wobbles from side to side each time either of them makes a move.

It has been two long days, the following one is to be even longer, and they are tired but determined to finish what they have begun.

Bright yellow lemon icing laces up Noah's fingers as he holds a piece of cake with one hand

and examines the game board at the same time.

They study the pattern of letters before them. They're impressed with the selections. Every word makes perfect sense.

They are each convinced that the other will win.

He looks at her and grins sheepishly, then takes a large bite of the cake, a few remaining crumbs glistening on his lips, the icing shining around two of his fingers like matching gold rings.

He's becoming such a handsome boy, Grace thinks to herself, resisting the temptation to touch his cheek. The boy's hair is growing in quickly, a deep golden brown, and it's clear that he's unused to its cover, often smoothing it with one hand.

And his color has also returned, now that of a normal boy. The flush in his cheeks seems natural, his sunken cheeks filled out, even his eyes appear larger, expressive, bright.

How she'd like to embrace him.

"I'm thirsty," he suddenly announces, finishing the cake with a single gulp and wiping his mouth with his sleeve.

"There's fresh milk in the fridge. Do you want me to get you a glass?"

"No, that's all right," he responds. "I'll just get it for myself. You have plenty of concentrating to do right here, anyway, if you have any intention of not forfeiting the game."

"Oh, I do, do I?"

They both laugh, and as Noah stands up his leg brushes the plate beside them, knocking it to the floor. The cake tumbles, then splits open into two long, jagged pieces, falling on the white carpet directly below.

Grace is reminded of a bouquet of bright tulips, yellow and red, spread open on the snowy tissue of a florist, just delivered from a wild summer garden, waiting to be watered and arranged.

His future is uncertain, she knows this, but she predicts great accomplishments to come.

She must leave soon. There will be other boys to care for. Other children, some even needier than him. Mrs. Saville had called the night before, promising that the grandmother's will identified a permanent guardian to take over, someone to make sure that Noah is protected until the age of eighteen.

As she leaves, she'll watch him wave to her from the window. His shadow will be unfaltering, his profile distinct, unmistakable. Later, she will be able to recognize him anywhere.

He'll be fine. He will grow into a healthy, strong young man. He will find a life without her, yet they will remain in close touch.

She will follow his progress carefully; she will visit him as often as he wants.

Others will be there to care for him, and he will provide for them in return.

He will have children of his own eventually. He will love and nourish them well.

He will think of Grace every so often.

He will speak of their days together fondly.

He will not be lost to her, nor her to him.

NOAH

The dark church is almost empty; few are there to help him say good-bye. And yet there are those who will reach out to him, those who will extend a helping hand, and among them he might even find his true double, a kindred spirit, someone to cling to while still walking a different path.

He knows this because she sits next to him, and he understands that when she is gone there will still be the two of them together: they will remain attached while also apart.

His heart is banging wildly, as if suddenly detached from its core, and he pictures it tumbling throughout his battered chest. The noise is so apparent, the sound of a loud knocking at some door that Noah finds himself wondering if anyone else can hear.

He looks at the woman beside him and fights the urge to reach for her hand. And then he suddenly thinks of his grandmother, how different she was from this friend.

He tries to remember the last time he saw his grandmother and suddenly has a vivid image of Mademoiselle.

She stood by the front door with a leather suitcase, her little sequined purse in one hand. How long since he had seen her upright, dressed and planning to go outside?

Recently, she had taken fewer and fewer pains with her own grooming, staying in bed all day and rarely fixing her dark, brittle hair. It would stick out straight around her face in a stiff semicircle, reminding him of a papier-mâché angel's cardboard halo, only black instead of white. Her makeup would be confused, off center, her expression appear somewhat half-crazed, and there would be dots of violet eyeshadow all over her caved-in, gaunt face. Her lips pursed into the size of a penny, when she spoke her skin would stretch and then collapse, and Noah would think of a child's toy accordion, opening and closing again and again.

He knew that she had been drinking, but never knew what to do. He understood that he couldn't say anything, that it was safer not to utter a word.

So the day she left for the hospital, determined to look young once more, Noah thought it a good opportunity for transformation, a possibility that she would also change within. She stood there, so fragile a creature, tiny, birdlike, leaning against the door, a red velvet beret covering her thinning hair.

She was wearing midnight blue suede pants that zipped at the ankle seam, fitting her body as tightly as a long winter glove. Her shoes were gold and pointed, the heels at least two inches high, and they bound her feet in a crisscrossed pattern, as if tying her permanently to both soles. Although it was summer, her black nylon sweater was buttoned all the way to her chin, and it had an iridescent sheen, appearing laced through and through with some kind of metal, silver or tin. When she moved, she would glisten and sparkle, but Noah knew that the glitter was fake, that it was only the stiff fabric that made each movement shimmer, the dark garment almost appearing alive.

She motioned to him with a crooked finger. She nodded, but at first didn't say a word. When he approached, he noticed she wasn't made up as usual, and was surprised by the beauty of her bare face. Her skin was pale, almost translucent, pure white without a mark of any kind, and it drooped down in folds like meringue batter, quivering each time she breathed. Noah bent forward so he could listen, but barely understood her last words.

Something about being careful. On the alert for unexpected turns of events. You can never be sure what will happen. You can never depend on others and must always watch out for yourself.

Stay on the lookout for burglars, my darling, or any intruders in the night. Strangers are not to be acknowledged, evil lurks at each and every street corner, you can never tell who might be planning to break in.

Lock everything up tightly. Pull the blinds,

dear, draw the curtains, stay inside. Don't forget to clean the refrigerator with Clorox, and make sure the freezer is making sufficient ice.

When I return the day after tomorrow, I expect to see everything in its place. Nothing changed, my dearest, my darling, not a single thing altered. Whose house is it, after all, who paid for each and every last thing?

If you wish, you can call the hospital later to see if the surgery is complete. Here's the number for the doctor and for someone who will eventually accompany me when I come home.

Don't open the door for anyone. Don't trust a soul, no matter what your instincts tell you, no matter what you think.

I have learned many things in my long life, and of this I am sure: it's easier to avoid calamity, my darling, if you never let anyone into your house.

The large room echoes, then is suddenly quiet, just the three of them and the pastor, no one else.

Will he be able to let go of his grandmother this final moment?

Will he have the courage to finally say good-bye?

No matter how accurate the line of sight, wind or human error is possible. No matter how vulnerable the target, it still can be left intact.

Tulips, the perfect colors, just as he had asked, and she remains right here beside him, as she promised, the steadfast, unforgettable, amazing Grace.

He looks up and for a moment feels desperate. What will happen, where is he to go, what will come next? Grace has assured him that he will be well cared for, and that she will be there to monitor each and every step. And yet, how strange it feels to continue alone without a shadow, without his double or his grandmother, Mademoiselle.

The porcelain urn seems make-believe, hard to imagine a human inside, his very own Mademoiselle.

But his grandmother was always tiny.

Small enough to be considered a child.

It seems sad to realize now that she never attained full growth.

Then he sees Grace looking, watching, anticipating his next move, and he rises, walking forward entirely on his own.

GRACE

the rustle of someone's dress behind her

grace
over here

fingers gripping the pew
lemon wax under her fingernails
its artificial scent making her sick

shh now, it will be all right

a blur of faces coming close
someone's powdered cheek
slowly brushing her own
dry dots of kisses stamping her face

    this is what she remembers of that day
    and tiny white gardenias
    draped over polished mahogany
    two brass handles on either side

Grace takes a deep breath and tries not to remember. This is Noah's day, his loss, not her own, and she must concentrate on helping him.

The boy sits wedged in between them, head down, hands folded in his lap, and she wonders if he would topple over if either she or Detective Hinkle should move.

They hold themselves erect, the three of them, hardly shifting position, in fact barely breathing at all. Perhaps it is because she is sitting so close to him, but for the first time since Grace has known Noah, she is aware of a boyish scent, musky and sweet, difficult to define. It's as if the tiniest pores of his skin have suddenly opened, releasing the sharp, unmistakable fragrance of youth ripening into adulthood. Grace can almost see a microscopic swatch of Noah's skin thickening before her eyes, and a mossy coat of the finest, downiest of hairs spreading over his arms. For a minute, she watches his chest widen, his torso lengthen, his entire body raise up from its skeleton like a ghostly apparition, then fall back into itself: settle, take root, and grow.

Now, in this most difficult of times, his grandmother's memorial, the boy seems to have stepped into his own shadow, somehow becoming whole, three-dimensional, growing up before her eyes.

Noah's sleeve brushes her own and he moves his arm quickly away. He's wearing a new suit that Grace bought for him the other day, navy with light pinstripes.

Noah leans forward and covers his face with both hands. How she would love to reach over and hug him, take his hand, stroke the back of his long neck. He stretches, head lowered, and then glances over his shoulder as if searching for someone's arrival, turning back to look directly at her.

For a moment, their eyes meet. His smile is sudden, uncertain, and his long black lashes wet. Grace reaches to touch him on the shoulder, but by then he has turned away again. The boy stands, then moves forward slowly, one step at a time.

And she herself, as well, will learn to step

ahead. She's already made the decision to call the number on the little scrap of paper she had initially thrown away, although it will be difficult, although it will take more courage than she ever knew she had. Maybe not tomorrow, maybe not even this month or next, but when Grace is ready, she will knock on a little girl's front door.

The parents may not be expecting her, they'll be surprised to see a stranger standing there. But the child will soon suddenly make an appearance, and nothing will ever be the same again. Grace will lean forward slowly, so as to look directly into her eyes. Then she'll recognize another. She'll be incredulous, stunned, dazed.

The whole family will hug her. They'll invite her through the open doorway. She won't hover at the entranceway, but will find her way all the way inside.

And then the four of them will sit down for dinner: mother, father, Grace, and little girl. The table will be set like no other, with a centerpiece of lush flowers, pink, purple, violet, and the polished silver glistening, crisp white linen napkins folded at every plate. Grace will be offered platters piled with the most dazzling food. The array of choices will stun her, she won't know exactly where to begin.

When it is time for her departure, she'll blow a kiss good-bye. But the little girl won't be satisfied and plead that she not go. Once again, Grace will lean over, this time taking the small face in both hands. She'll whisper that they're now related and will feast together once again soon. Leaving's never easy. It's always difficult to say good-bye.

Although their features are not identical, she shares a heart with this child.

Grace looks up and sees Noah waiting. He holds out his hand and looks about to speak. And then she realizes that it's all over. The ceremony has ended.

The grieving complete.

CHANGE

The symbols of change represent the strength of our nature
and our ability to incorporate transition and challenge
in our life while maintaining the very core of our being.

· EPILOGUE ·

NOAH

Where does my life go from here? Like everyone else, I am unsure.

Will Grace fall in love with Detective Hinkle, will they marry and adopt me, a nuclear family for the rest of our lives?

I doubt it.

But Mademoiselle left me an impressive inheritance, more money than I could ever expect, and had the foresight to make her lawyer my guardian. I prefer things this way, I really do. I am not meant to be one of many; I am already one of two.

Perhaps I will decide on boarding school, an exclusive one in New England, only the best. I imagine large libraries filled with leather-bound volumes; I can see myself reading at a long, wooden carved desk.

There I will finish the preparations for my mysterious future life.

Grace will surely visit me on weekends, swinging large straw bags filled with cookies and the small chocolate almond cakes that bring me such delight. We will make a picnic on the lawn, her soft charcoal-gray sweater spread out like a shadow on the grass, its sleeves extended and providing warmth from beneath. She will hand me a slice of chocolate on wax paper, her fingers smudged from the glistening fudge, her face illuminated with expectation. I will take a small bite at first, savoring the rich, complex flavors of the savory and the sweet, and then finish it quickly, perhaps even asking for more.

Maybe Grace will tell me about her own dead boy, how they were parted forever and yet found each other again. Maybe she will never tell me this.

It doesn't matter; somehow I already know. I have seen the photograph, I have heard her silence, I have recognized her sorrow. Strange how that which is hidden will make itself known.

Eventually it will get chilly. The wind will pick up and blow.

Grace will laugh as Mademoiselle's red beret spins and races over the golden autumn grass. We will find it later.

Come evening, we will say good-bye.

I will head back to the large dormitory, where the boys still ignore me or call me dreadful names. But then I will glance back at Grace as she disappears down the lawn, and taste the bit of chocolate still clinging to my tongue. I will know that she will return.

I have learned little in my short life, but there are a few things I do know. It may be necessary to be separated by circumstance, even detached at your very bone, but it is also possible to remain conjoined, permanently rooted at the soul.

We are the rarest of human beings, thoracopagus, fixed, born sharing one heart.

There was only one heart between us.

I lived.

THE UNIVERSE

The universe represents the cycle of life in which we experience
death and birth, success and failure, along with courageous growth.
The end of a journey has finally arrived and yet a new path beckons.

The sands whispered, *Be separate,*
the stones taught me, *Be hard.*
I dance, for the joy of surviving,
on the edge of the road.

— Stanley Kunitz, "An Old Cracked Tune"

· ACKNOWLEDGMENTS ·

There are many friends who have helped bring this small book to life. Thank you to my friend and agent, Anne Edelstein; my extraordinary, insightful, loyal editor, Katherine Tegen; the devoted Julie Hittman; and all those at HarperCollins who tended to my manuscript with sensitivity and care.

Thank you to my cherished colleagues at American University who quietly and consistently support my work, especially my beloved friend, Leah Johnson, for reading early drafts, along with the writers Carolyn Parkhurst and Barbara Esstman.

With deep respect for Anne Adelman, who delicately and tenaciously has entered my interior life.

Thank you to Donna Greenfield, generous and enduring friend.

And to Twig George, always my first and most enthusiastic reader.

I also appreciate the help of Peggy Anderson and John M. Templeton, Jr., M.D., without whom my medical research would have been impossible.

Thank you to my remarkable daughters, Jennifer and Lisa, who teach humility and courage.

And with appreciation for my mother, Julia K. Gosliner, during her first daring years in a new world.